BLOOM

SHAIDA ESCOFFERY

DEDICATION

To Mikaela: Never stop growing, never stop blooming, never stop believing. Thank you for being the Ellie I've always needed.
To DJ: Your crisis helped me believe more now than ever. Don't be afraid to start over. I think we both hit the reset button this year. Thank God for fresh starts.

CONTENTS

ACKNOWLEDGMENTS

The love, faithfulness, and goodness of God is so overwhelming that billions of pages of thanks wouldn't be enough. I am forever grateful for his patience with me and for all the people that he's placed in my life to water the seeds he has planted in my life.

To my family, thank you for your unwavering support and for always being a safe place every time I felt discouraged. You have celebrated every victory with me, big or small.

My friends and church family span all over the US and they have all helped shape this journey in my life. Thank you for every laugh and even the hard conversations.

I am blooming because of you.

1

She was the type of old lady to strike up a conversation with anyone. How's work? How's your family? Is there anyone special in your life?

The questions got deeper and more invasive the more you talked, so let's just say I wasn't exactly enthusiastic when I was asked to carry Sister Blossom Titus to church and back home each Sunday. She went by a couple of names: Sister Blossom, Sister B, Sister Titus and the twins called her, Sister T.

I thought it couldn't get worse until they gave all the old ladies an assignment as soon as March started: pick a group of five young women and teach them. Sister Titus took those verses in Titus very seriously. This was her namesake. So now, not only did I spend Sundays with her, but Wednesdays after work, and she texted us every day!

The only bright point of this whole thing was that she also chose my best friend Ellie to be in this group and Rachel and I used to be close. At least I had someone else to share this burden with. So it was me (Autumn), Ellie, Camila and Valentina (the twins), and Rachel.

"She can't be that bad, Autumn," Ellie said as we made our way to the car to go pick up Sister Blossom for church. Ellie had spent the night at my house and now she would have to join me for my Sunday morning routine.

"Reserve your opinion after she bombards you with questions."

I was right, as Sister Titus made her way to the car; I braced myself. She had skin the color of toffee and even though she was filled with wrinkles and her hands were leathery and veined, she looked strong. She had long white hair that she pulled back into a bun. I imagined that when she was younger she must've been really pretty. But, she'd told me she'd never been married and had no kids.

On her thin frame a bright pink skirt suit paired with white stockings and white flats. *Lord, please help me not to dress like that when I get old*, I said silently to myself. In no less than two minutes into the drive she started her line of interrogation with Ellie.

"So, Ellie, how's the family?"

I saw Ellie's eyes dart to mine before she answered, "They're fine."

"I haven't seen your sister in a while."

Ellie used her finger to fix her glasses. "She's… uh, she's out of town."

"She's been away for a while. Did she get a job somewhere else?"

"I suppose so."

"You suppose?"

I chimed in. "Yeah, she's so busy these days Ellie can hardly keep up with her." I put on my indicator and made a left turn onto the next road. The faster I can get us to the church was the faster this interrogation would be over.

"Well tell her to remember this is home. We all miss her."

"I'll make sure to tell her."

Ellie's older sister Emmy packed her bags and left three months ago. I mean she had been going back and forth from home and wherever for months, but she would always still at least come to church on the weekends. But, three months ago Ellie and her family had come home to see all of Emmy's stuff gone and a few of their valuables too. No one knows the whole story, only Emmy could tell us that, but we do know that it started with stealing painkillers out the cabinet, just a few, and then eventually that couldn't do it. Emmy, the girl that taught me how to apply my foundation properly and promised to do my makeup on my big day disappeared into the night searching for heroin and never came home. She left a note explaining that she didn't want to come back and cops don't go searching for people who don't want to be found.

Ellie and I prayed about it all the time. There wasn't much I could do for her except pray, listen and give her a scripture when she needed it. I couldn't promise her that her sister would come back. There was a possibility they could get a call that she was dead. But, I do believe her sister will come back. I have to believe that. Plus, it's much easier believing for someone else than for myself.

"I got lots to pray about then," Sister Titus said, "Emmy, a baby for Ms. Rachel, for the twins to get scholarships for college and for you Ms. Autumn we're praying for a nice young man to come scoop you up."

Ellie smirked at me and flipped her box braids over her shoulder. I chuckled. "Sister Titus save your prayers for the others."

I shouldn't have been so surprised when in the meeting Sister Titus handed each of us a small bag with a paper attached.

"Inside each bag are seeds. I want you all to plant your seed in your backyard, or front yard if you choose. But before you do, I want us to pray over them. Think of each seed as the thing you desire the most right now. The thing you would want God to bring to pass. Pray for that and think of the process of the seed growing from a seedling to full bloom as the same process for your miracle. It won't be overnight. But something will be happening in the soil from the moment you plant it and every day you can choose to water it or neglect it."

"Are all of the seeds the same type of plant?" Camila asked, her brunette curls bouncing.

"No," Sister Titus said. "But I won't tell you what type of plant it is. That's up to you to discover through patience."

"My plant is gonna die. I don't have a green thumb," I said, shaking my head and laughing.

She smiled, "Autumn, don't let your words kill your prayer."

I wanted to tell her that I didn't say anything about my prayer. I only mentioned my plant. But, I kept quiet.

"Now, we all know this is a safe place. What's said here, stays here. So, would anyone like to share their prayer requests?"

Of course, the twins' hands shot up simultaneously. "We both want full rides to Georgetown, because we both want to go to law school and become human rights lawyers," Camila said. Even though Camila and Valentina had identical curly brown tresses, pale skin, and brown eyes, and the same voice, it seemed that I always knew the difference between the two when they opened their mouth. Camila was always making orders while Valentina seemed content to just sit back and watch.

I had to hold myself back from rolling my eyes. How quaint that both of them wanted to do the exact same thing. Rachel spoke up next. "Keith and I have been trying to have a baby for years. The doctors say it's impossible." Even I stopped and looked over at the girl who used to be my roommate for all four years of college. The Rachel I knew had the brightest smile that made her green eyes glitter and glow and now she looked…tired. Like all the life was drained out of her, her hair was thin and a dull mousy brown. Guilt twisted my stomach into a knot, why had I never noticed this until now?

"Not even IVF?" Ellie asked.

"IVF won't work. The problem isn't my ability to conceive. It's to carry," Rachel answered, her voice quavering.

There seemed to be a hush in the room, I couldn't imagine her pain. Now I really didn't want to speak up at all. How do you follow that?

"We will bring that to God in prayer Rachel," Sister Blossom said. "Ellie.?"

"Pray that my sister gets clean and comes home."

I stared at Ellie. She'd never publically told anyone about her sister being an addict. We all knew her sister was MIA, but no one else knew why.

Everyone nodded silently and then I could feel all the eyes on me. "Autumn?" Sister Blossom said.

Was I really gonna tell them my prayer request? That right now what I wanted felt like the most pathetic thing in the world? "Umm, just pray for a deeper walk with Christ."

Sister Blossom looked at me like she knew all my secrets. I don't know how to explain it, that small smile where you know she knows, but you hope she doesn't know for real, so you're not about to make her feel like she knows. And, of course Ellie was giving me that look that read: Really?!

"Ok, before we pray I just want you guys to follow my instructions carefully. Do you all promise to do everything exactly as I tell you?"

Everyone agreed loudly while I softly gave my vow. She continued, "Follow the instructions of how to plant your seeds and care for them strictly. If you don't, you will not see your plant grow. Pray and read the word each and every day. There's a rotation I would like you to follow. Autumn, I would like you to lead this group. You'll help each person plant their-

"Whoa…whoa…um," I laughed sarcastically. "Sister Blossom, I told you I don't have a green thumb. I don't think I'm the right person."

"Well a couple people didn't think they were the right person either. Look at Moses, Gideon, or even Esther," she responded.

What in the world was I supposed to say back to that? I sighed in frustration. She came over and tapped my shoulder lightly. "You'll be fine, my dear," she said before laying out further instructions. "Autumn you'll help Ellie plant hers first, then Valentina, then Camila, and then Rachel."

"Don't they live at the same place? Can't I just do theirs at the same time?"

"No, they're two separate people. Two separate plants. Two separate times."

Camila protested, "Well, then Valentina's will grow before mine."

"If it does, then it does."

For the first time I wanted to high five Sister Blossom for something she said. Let me not speak too quickly because I'm sure she'll do something soon to make me change my mind.

"Let's pray," she said. "Lord, I place all these desires before you. We believe by faith that you are able to accomplish your divine will in each of these women's lives. For some they will get exactly what they asked for, but for some you may unfold a different plan. Help them to accept all that comes with this journey. Grace them with the strength they need. Most importantly Lord, change them so that they are ready to embrace your plans. In Jesus Name, Amen."

"Amen," we all said.

"Wait, Sister Blossom, if Autumn's helping us, who's gonna help plant hers?" Ellie asked.

"I will, of course," she said. "Autumn and I have lots to discuss."

Yeah, there it was…the thing I knew was gonna make me change my mind.

2

"What was up with you?" Ellie asked me Friday after work as we plunged our shovels into the earth. Our friendship was so unconventional. We weren't even close to the same age, she was five years younger, a girl with box braids I had been assigned to mentor, who now had become more like a little sister.

"What do you mean?"

"Just pray for a deeper walk with Christ," she said mocking me. She had taken off her glasses and kept squinting.

"What's wrong with that? Shouldn't I ask for that?" I said, stabbing my shovel against the dirt.

"Yes, but you were being fake," she said as she mimicked my harsh digging.

I put the shovel down. "Fake?" I could feel the grit of the soil in the creases of my hands and underneath my fingernails.

"Yes, fake. Aren't you always the one telling me to tell the truth no matter what, to not care what anyone thinks of me?"

I sighed and turned away. "What was I supposed to say after Rachel talked about not being able to have a baby and you talked about Emmy? Am I really supposed to say, 'Hey everyone, pray for me to get a husband?'"

"Sure, why not?"

"No," I said definitively, picking back up my shovel and digging. "Plus, I told you and Sister B, we can save those prayers for everyone else. It's just me and God right now. That's it. He's all I need."

"You're lying. Maybe you've been lying to yourself so much that you're starting to believe it. You didn't share your request because 'He's all you need'. You don't think God can do it. And if you don't think he can do it, maybe you don't know him as well as you think you do."

I shook my head. "So now you know motives?"

"No. But, I know you Autumn."

"Ok, so what do you want me to do Ellie?" I asked,

dusting off the dirt onto the old jeans I was wearing.

"Try."

"Don't you think I've tried?"

"You haven't tried this?"

"What is this? Planting trees with an old lady to keep her busy? Come on El, you don't seriously think this could work?"

"Yeah, I do. I think it can. It's worth a try."

I still thought this was dumb. But, I didn't want to discourage her. I sighed in frustration. "Ok, ok, I'll try for you."

"No, don't try for me. Try for you. I think there's a lot we can learn about ourselves through this. Doesn't God say our faith is like a seed?"

"Planting is easy Ellie, taking care of it each day is hard. Which is why I don't want to start this whole seed thing in the first place." I squatted down and started to use a smaller shovel.

"Are you talking about the seed or your faith?" she asked.

I flicked a crumb of dirt from under my nail. "Would you judge me if I said both?"

"Judge you, no. Tell you that you're wrong, yes."

"I don't want to start anything I can't finish," I said pulling my dark brown hair into a bun. I looked down at my skin on my hands that was blending with the color of the soil.

"You're afraid," she said drawing the bag of seeds out. "What are you afraid of Autumn?"

"What does fear have to do with this Ellie?" I said, sitting down, my legs tired of squatting. "I'm just saying that when I plant mine, I'll probably forget to water it and it'll die, and then I'll feel bad cause I'm gonna be a tree killer."

She rolled her eyes. "You're overthinking, which means you're anxious and anxiety means there's something you fear."

"Sheesh. Thank you for the psychoanalysis." I dusted off my hands as I saw her pull out a note from her bag of seeds. "She put a note in there? What does it say?" I asked.

"And let us not be weary in well doing: for in due season we shall reap, if we faint not. Galatians 6:9."

"So basically, this seed is going to be an endurance thing," I said.

"Well, I've been enduring for this long with Emmy. Why not? What do I have to lose?"

Ellie poured the bag of seeds into the ground. The seeds looked like little circular pods to me. "Do you know what type of plant it is?" I asked.

"Nope."

"Don't you want to look it up?"

"Sister Blossom said not to."

"And you're not curious?"

"Of course, I am. But, I promised to follow all her directions."

I laughed. "Why do I feel like everyone is drinking from the kool-aid except me?"

"Cause you're too afraid of being a tree killer, or maybe just scared of believing."

I rolled my eyes. "Ok El, want to know what I'm afraid of? I'm afraid of disappointment. I'm afraid to go hard again praying for this thing and be disappointed again. So, planting some symbolic tree isn't gonna change that. Cause I can try my hardest and that tree could still die, so why bother?"

She stared at me. "Is that what you think about my sister?"

"What?" I asked, meeting her eyes. "Come on El, you know I'm not talking about Em. That's totally different."

"No, it's not. What's different between my prayer and your prayer?"

"It's different."

"How?"

"I don't know!" I yelled. "It just is," I said softly. I could feel the sting of tears. "I don't want to talk about this right now."

She nodded. "Ok." She quietly started to cover the hole where the seeds fell from her bag with the dirt. I joined her in covering the space with soil.

Ellie sighed and started to pray. "Lord, I pray that as we plant this seed in faith that this plant, whatever it may be will grow to be a living testament to your ability to bring life into this world and into the dead places in our lives. Whether it is a flower, a tree, or a vine, I pray that you will use the growth of this plant to teach me some very valuable lessons about you. I believe that one day my sister will be back home with me to see whatever this plant will grow to be, and I believe that as Autumn has planted with me that you will give her the strength to plant her own seed knowing that she doesn't have to have all the strength to last the journey right now, but just enough to walk by faith moment by moment in Jesus name, amen."

I quietly said amen. Then she poured some water on the mound.

I cleared my throat. "I have to go home now. Gotta get some rest."

Ellie's only reply was "Mmmm hmmm."

I stood up and wiped my hands on my dirty jeans. "Well, I'll see you tomorrow, aren't we gonna watch a movie tomorrow?"

"No," she said, reaching into her pocket and pulling out a folded piece of paper. "Sister Blossom said to give you this."

"What?" I said with a voice mixed with surprise and annoyance as I took the paper and opened it.

Thank you for following through with your promise to help Ellie plant her seed. I knew you would feel comfortable working with her first and that she would encourage you for your next step to plant your own seed. I will see you tomorrow at six. We have a lot to discuss as we plant your seed. I'm looking forward to seeing you.

Blossom Titus

I wish I could say that I slept that night, but I didn't. I wasn't looking forward to Sister Blossom's visit, to planting this tree, but I really wasn't looking forward to the questions, the questions Ellie asked and the one's I'm sure Sister Blossom would ask. Questions I didn't want to answer.

3

When I was younger all I wanted to be was older. I just couldn't wait for the day when life would begin. When I could make my own decisions, start a career I loved, get married, have kids, live the American dream. But it's funny how no one tells you that this dream turns you into a windchaser like Solomon warns. Maybe they did tell me. I probably wasn't listening.

During high school I was a nerd, the living definition of an awkward black girl, not like the nerds on TV that got beat up, but the nerd that truly only cared about having good grades and being successful. I could care less about popularity and I really didn't care which guy did or didn't like me. Not that anyone ever really liked me in high school, not to my knowledge anyhow.

I guess I could see through the façade of most of these high school relationships. I'm with you because you make me feel good about myself and increase my popularity, and we probably like the same rapper or band, or maybe you're the guy my parents told me not to date and I want to irritate them. It was all pointless to me. In a few weeks or months, it would end. Even those who made it to the end eventually said their goodbyes once it was time to go to college. At the end of the day, they both realized it was emotional and fun, and they probably shared their lives and bodies with each other, their verbal commitments weren't enough. There was a new phase of life waiting for them with more fishes in the sea. So, no, I wasn't the type to meet my one true love at 15.

I was more open to love in college and there was someone I once thought I loved, but I don't really think I did. Of course, I said it, I believed it at the time. Wholeheartedly. But maybe I was more in love with love itself. The rush of emotions. The thrill of having someone think that you're captivating. But when you're just starting college you're just like a high schooler, just in a new environment and so I don't think I was much different than the high schoolers I rolled my eyes at. I just thought I was, cause now I had autonomy over a few more areas of my life.

That relationship crashed and burned leaving me with a few scars: trust issues, additional self-esteem issues, but with the biggest lesson of all: never do anything again outside of God's will. So, I tried my hardest not to. For the rest of my college career I avoided any guys that I knew God wouldn't be happy if I dated. The one's that explicitly told me they wanted to hook up, the ones that pretended to actually want to know me before eventually asking me to hookup with them, and the ones who wanted to brag to all their friends that they'd gotten the Christian girl.

Oh yes, college was an enlightening time indeed. I learned how to sift out the good from the bad quickly. I could tell when a guy had a girlfriend, even though he was still flirting with me and asking for my number. I could tell when a guy was lying that he 'loved Jesus" to get close to me. I learned how to ask the right questions, friendly, subtly, but quickly. Oh, I learned.

And when college was over I was a 22-year-old on my way to grad school, thinking that my new acquired knowledge of all the men to avoid could help me. Except no one told me that you don't learn how to tell a counterfeit by hanging out with counterfeits. Bank tellers know the real from the fake because they know how a real bill looks and feels. Talk about the miseducation of the church girl.

So, let me tell you what happened from 22 until now. I kept getting friend zoned. Why? I wish I could completely answer that. But, I suppose it might be because I thought so much like a guy, so I could spot the bad dudes, that men only saw me as a girl who could be their dude, not their girl. I'm not saying this is the only reason, I think if I had this thing figured out, I wouldn't be turning 28 and still have men saying, "I'm just not attracted to you in that way" or "ahhhhhh I think we'd be cool just staying friends, you're my dawg, I don't wanna lose that." But the best ones are the liars who say dumb stuff like "You're too good for me."

If you've been paying close attention you'll definitely see that another problem is that guys are the ones turning me down, not the other way around. Basically, guys don't really ask me out. I'm always the one revealing my feelings only to get the easy let down cause they're afraid to hurt my feelings. Ellie tells me I should stop saying that guys don't ask me out cause that's not true, ok, let me amend that…Sane men don't ask me out. I think I've gotten two proposals, both from drunks.

And so, if you ask me, although being in a loving relationship, putting on a stunning white dress, cooking meals for my husband and seeing my body change as I provided a home for new life, mattered the most to me…I'm over it. I will be an auntie, a godmother, a bridesmaid forever. But, I will not put myself in a position to be told that I am not good enough ever again. I will not tell anyone of the loneliness that grips me at times like a vice. That I cry each time I see another fairy tale unfolding for another person, not tears of joy for them, but tears of pity for myself. Or how my frustration and anger is slowly choking me like a python. I seem to be angry at men, but I am not. I am angry with God. I am so angry, and I don't want to be, but I don't know how to stop.

When my doorbell rang, and I looked outside to see Sister Blossom on my porch, I thought about lying and telling her I was too sick, so we had to cancel this little planting session. It's Saturday, I should be sleeping in, going out on the town, running errands, or even catching up on laundry, not planting trees with a nosy senior citizen. Despite what you may already think about me, I'm not that mean. I may think mean things, but I'd never actually say or do them.

I opened the door and gave a pleasant smile. "Good afternoon Sister Titus."

She stood there and smiled back before saying, "Good afternoon, Autumn. I'm very happy to see you even though I know you probably wish I would just leave you alone to enjoy your Saturday."

I should've said, "You just read my mind." But instead I opted for a veiled lie. "Oh, don't say that, come inside Sister Titus." Once she was inside, I closed the door and said, "Let me get my gloves and shovel." No use in prolonging this meeting. I was ready to get this thing over with. Once I got the stuff out my garage, I joined her back in the living room where I'd left her.

"Are you ready?" I asked her. But, she seemed caught up in her own thoughts looking around at the different pictures on my walls and the décor.

"You have a beautiful home," she said quietly.

"Thank you."

"Did you decorate it yourself?"

"Yes, I did. Well my family helped paint and move in furniture when I first moved out on my own, but I did most of the decorating myself." Once I finished grad school, I had used my first year of working to save up to buy this two-bedroom townhouse in Doral. It was hard work to save so much during that time, but I'd done it and I was proud of my spot. I remember when everyone had come by to help me paint it in golden and auburn colors.

"Do you enjoy living here alone?"

I bit down on my lip. "I don't mind it. It's quiet and when I want it loud I can sing or play my music as loud as I want."

She continued to look around and spotted painting of autumn leaves on the wall. "That's a gorgeous painting. I love the colors of fall."

I chuckled lightly. "I didn't expect you to like autumn."

"Why not?"

"Well, you love flowers and plants, your name is Blossom. You sound like more of a spring lover, not Autumn when everything is dying."

Her eyes widened in surprise. "Is that you what you think of your name?"

"I don't think much of my name. I didn't have a choice in it." It was true. I liked my name, I just didn't think on it much.

"Autumn shows us the cycle of seasons that there can be a beauty even in things that are dying. Because do you know what's happening during autumn when the leaves are falling? They're also dropping seeds into the ground. Seeds that go down into the ground and die, bringing new life during spring."

I chuckled sarcastically this time. "Well, you'll see over this project that the most I'll be good for is dropping these seeds into the ground."

"You don't like me very much do you Autumn?"

I was expecting her to ask me another question, but I sure wasn't expecting that one. "Why would you say that?" I asked incredulously.

"You haven't answered," she said. I opened my mouth to answer but she spoke again. "Let me stop you before you lie to an old lady. I know you don't like me very much. I'm old, but not stupid. I also know you could care less about planting that seed."

I felt flushed, flustered, and if I could think of another synonym I felt that too. "I...I... I just think this might not be the best use of my time."

She nodded. "Do you know why I chose you Autumn?"

"Excuse me?"

"Why I chose you for my group. You were my very first choice."

"I thought those groups were selected randomly."

"Well the other ladies said they had no preference and selected randomly. I said I want to work with Autumn, Ellie, Rachel, Valentina and Camila."

Now I really had no words. I only put up with this because I thought this was some random selection by the Ladies' ministry and now she's telling me that she planned this all along. "And why would you choose me?"

"Since I came to Harvest Community two years ago, I've paid close attention to you, every Sunday you go up there and you sing and sometimes I see the tears come down your face," she said, placing her hand on mine while I remained stiff to her touch. "But those tears are not the tears everyone thinks they are." She placed a hand on my cheek. "And those smiles you smile are not real smiles. You see, everything is always in the eyes my dear."

She took her time and went over to the table where I had the bag with the seeds. "And so, I knew the other girls needed their seeds. But, you really needed it."

I was not touched. I was angry. Angry that she had read me like a neon sign, when I thought I had done an expert job at concealing myself. "So, are you going to tell me now that I'm unhappy because I'm single? Since that seems to be what you're always getting at."

She laughed as if I had said something silly. "No. Of course not. That would be ridiculous."

She continued. "You are unhappy because you don't know God."

"Excuse me?" I hissed.

"Those that know their God, put their trust in him."

I could feel the sting of tears. I was so angry I could burst, but yet I found myself unable to unleash my anger on her. Call it my upbringing, about respecting elders, but I stayed silent, internally wrestling with the thought of tossing her out. She was right, but I hated it. I HATED it.

She came over and placed her hand on my shoulder. "Oh, Autumn you are so burdened down. This is not what God wants for you."

She walked past me to the sliding glass door and opened it and stepped outside. "Come on, I know you want to just get this over with and get rid of me."

I followed her outside still not saying a word. She walked over to the middle of my backyard and took a deep breath. "Right here, you can start digging right here." I walked over to the spot and started digging still remaining mute. Then she started to sing.

"I must tell Jesus all of my trials, I cannot bear these burdens alone; In my distress He kindly will help me, he ever loves and cares for his own."

I pretended to ignore her as she sang until she said, "Oh, Autumn you're a much better singer than me. Why don't you sing it?"

"I'm not in a singing mood Sister Titus," I said, continuing my digging.

"Come on, it'll help the time go by faster," she said and I wanted to roll my eyes at this lady in her mom jeans and ugly floral top.

"Is there some kind of special way to put these seeds in the ground?" I asked, still ignoring her request for me to sing.

"Nope, just scatter them a bit. You don't want to just

pile them on top of each other." She returned to her request. "So, are you going to sing?"

I wanted her to shut up. So, as I scattered the seed across the wide plain of dirt I dug up, I started to sing, "I must tell Jesus all of my trials, I cannot bear these burdens alone; In my distress He kindly will help me, he ever loves and cares for his own." But as I hit the refrain, I could feel the heaviness in my voice, tremors from my heart and throat flowing down to my hands as I struggled to choke out the words.

"I must Jesus! I must tell Jesus!"

The next line came out in a heavy sigh. "I cannot bear my burdens alone."

The next were heaving sobs as I said "I must tell Jesus! I must tell Jesus! Jesus can help me, Jesus alone."

I felt Sister Blossom's hand on my shoulder. As I clung to my shovel and tightly shut my eyes. I don't like to cry in front of people. I don't like to feel weak. Not in front of friends, family, Sister Blossom or even God.

"He's listening Autumn. He's listening." I couldn't look at her. I was so embarrassed.

"I'm sorry. I'm not usually like this," I said still weeping uncontrollably.

"Yes, I know." She took the shovel from me and started to finish off the work of covering the hole. This lady should've needed a cane or walker, but she was handling that shovel like a teenager in their prime. She finished and looked at me once more. "I chose you because you needed to see that in order to plant a seed you must have faith that the ground can produce something. Without faith Autumn, it is impossible to please God, for he that cometh to God must believe that he is and that he is a rewarder of them that diligently seek him." She put down the shovel and took both my hands in hers. "Friction from years of pain has a way of making the most delicate of hearts callous. So, someone must come and dig it up and plant there and water there, then life will come back again into the Earth."

Tears were dropping into my mouth. "I don't know how to not feel this way."

"Sure, you do, you just sang it."

4

I spent the next few days thinking about what really happened that day. How did my anger turn into this overwhelming helplessness? How did I end up sobbing on Sister Blossom's shoulder accepting my next assignment to help Valentina, then Camila, and then Rachel plant their seeds?

Did I feel better after that day? Yes, I must admit I did. Somehow lighter. It was the first I ever told anyone how frustrated I was with God, how I couldn't understand what he was doing and why. All I wanted to know was why and I couldn't get an answer to that question. I couldn't say that God wasn't good. My head told me he was. It was my heart that had doubts. And I told Sister Blossom. Let me repeat that for you, I didn't tell Ellie that because I wouldn't want to be a bad example, I wouldn't want to ruin her faith. I didn't tell my parents or my leaders at church, cause they'd just lecture me and rebuke me for my lack of trust. I told Sister Blossom. The person it made the least sense for me to tell.

She didn't rebuke me. She wasn't harsh. She listened mostly. And then she handed me a journal and told me to start praying in it, starting that day. Tell God everything. She told me to use my voice to sing from where I am, but also where I need to be. And you know what? I think Ellie might be right.

Sister Blossom isn't so bad.

Telling God felt hard. I suppose it was like putting peroxide on cut. It stung, but the next day I felt better. I told him how I didn't understand, and how mad that made me. How I was so frozen in this place that I could hardly feel him anymore. I told him that I knew I was living like a fraud because every week I got up and led worship at my church. Every week, I went up and told people to believe God, to trust him. I told them about Peter sinking the moment he took his eyes off Jesus. I told them how Sarah laughed and tried to create her own methods of solving the problem and created a mess. I told them of how Mary readily accepted God's will even in the midst of danger. I told them how David slayed a giant through faith, how Gideon defeated an army, yet I only "trusted" in the moment. After I left church I succumbed to my own negative thoughts that told me that this faith thing hadn't worked and would never work.

I was honest. In those prayers, did the heavens open up and send down a reply? No. But, I slept easier that night. Even though I didn't understand any more than I did before. Somehow telling God was enough for now.

Until I realized that God was ready to speak, or maybe I finally started to listen.

I met with the twins four days after planting my own seeds. I never minded going to their house. Their abuela always had food, and some crazy novella on. Or at least Caso Cerrado. Did I understand everything her abuela said to me? No. All those years of Spanish and when Abuela gets mad and starts speaking at a rapid pace, I'm good if I understood five words. But, my assumption is that she likes me, based on the food of course.

As I stepped outside in the backyard with Valentina, Camila stuck her head outside. "Why did Valé get to go first?"

I rolled my eyes. "Because that's what's on Sister Blossom's schedule. So go back inside and when I'm done with Valé, I'll call you out here."

Camila rolled her eyes and went back inside. I turned to Valentina. "Is she always like this?"

She laughed. "Yeah." She tucked a stray curl behind her ear. "Camila's always been the more competitive twin. It's either we do it together or she does it first."

"Does it bother you a lot?"

She played with the dirt on the ground with the front end of her boot. "I mean sometimes. I'm just not really into competing you know. Plus, I always lose to Camila with everything."

"What do you mean that you lose to her?"

"Well, her GPA is higher than mine and Mami, Papi and Abuela are always saying why can't you keep your room clean like Camí, why can't you do this or that like Camí and all the guys like her."

"If the guys think she's cute, don't you think they think you're cute too?"

"Well, they don't. Camí is just...she's the better twin."

I felt like I was in the twilight zone. Could someone's self-esteem be so warped that they couldn't see that they looked exactly like the person they aspired to be? "Valentina there's obviously no physical differences between you and your sister. It took me years to even be able to tell you guys apart. When you don't have confidence, it shows."

"But Camila-

"Ok, let's not talk about Camila. Who are you? What do you want for yourself? Who would you want to be if you weren't a twin?"

She looked at me, her brown eyes pensive and serious. "I don't know. I really don't know."

I'm not sure if it was my training kicking in or if it was something else entirely. "Do you even want to go to Georgetown? Do you want to be a lawyer?"

I saw a tear trail down her cheek. She gave a shaky reply. "No, I don't."

"So, what do you want do?"

She wiped at her face. "I want to go to design school. I got accepted into Parsons, you know the famous school in New York."

My eyes widened. "Valentina, that's fantastic! How

come you didn't tell me?"

She shrugged. "I didn't tell anyone. I just wanted to see if I'd actually get in. It doesn't make a difference though. No one wants me to be a designer, making dresses for prom is cool and everything, but they want me to have a real job and to go to school with Camila. We've never been apart."

My heart bled for her, I understood what it was like to not believe in yourself, to think you were less than, to be so confused about what you wanted to do and who you wanted to be because you'd always been trying to be someone else. I saw myself when I was 17 just like her and realized maybe not much had changed since then. Somehow, I knew God was speaking to me, and that I needed these words just as much as she did. "Listen to me, you are beautiful, and competent, you are a unique individual."

I picked up the bag of seeds on the ground and pulled out a few. "Your seeds are different than your sister's for a reason, cause although you guys may look the same, you're not the same. You have different personalities, thoughts, dreams, and a different calling. Do you want to live your whole life miserable cause you're living Camila's dream? Or do you want to live the dream that God placed inside of you?"

She wiped away a tear and played with a loose curl. "You're right." She smirked. "I bet they're all gonna flip when I tell them."

I nodded, "Yeah, you're probably right. How fast do you think your abuela will start speaking in Spanish?"

"Reina del drama!"

I laughed. "Just like her novelas."

"Sí, just like her novelas." She cleared her throat. "I feel like you're good at this."

"Good at what?" I asked confused.

She stood in front of me. "Being sure of yourself. Knowing what you want. Standing up for yourself. You know being confident."

I laughed again, "Can I tell you a secret? I literally cry once a week thinking that I'm not enough, not pretty enough, that I'll never accomplish the dreams that I have for myself."

"What are your dreams?"

I didn't know if I would tell her the truth or maybe just the veiled answers I had given everyone for years. "I'm a college counselor, but did you know what I really wanted to do. I wanted to just create music, write songs, perform them. Tell people about Jesus. But, I was too scared of rejection and so I gave up, and I wanted to be a wife and a mom more than anything else and I can't even get a date. So yeah, there's been plenty of times I have cried myself to sleep just wondering why am I not good enough or pretty enough."

"I honestly thought it was just me."

I chuckled. "Me too." I looked over at the plot of open space by her fence. "Why don't we plant over there?"

"Yeah, that's a good spot."

We both made our way over there and started the work of digging, the smell of fresh earth greeting us as we buried the seeds in the soil and covered it. Valentina poured water on the mound. "Did you look up what your seed is?" she asked.

"No, did you?"

"I tried to, but it was too complicated to find," she said bashfully.

"Curiosity got the best of you."

"Yeah, it did. Camila looked up hers."

"Did she find it?"

"Yeah, it's ivy. She wasn't too happy about it. She wanted something prettier she said."

I smirked, "Well, then I guess it's time to bring Camila out here so we can plant hers and she can tell me all about it."

Valentina laughed cheerfully, "Good luck," she said as she made her way over to the door of the house. "Hey, Autumn, if I go to design school will you promise to let me make your wedding dress someday?"

Wedding dress? Didn't she just hear me tell her that I couldn't get a date? She'd probably wear a wedding dress before I did. But, I wasn't going to burst her bubble. Or maybe I didn't want her to know how much I'd really given up. So, I said, "It's a tough job. Do you think you're up to it?"

She nodded. "I can do it."

I smiled. "Well, since you're so sure, surprise me."

5

Camila came outside with all her gear: gloves, various shovels and pots. "I looked it up and it says that ivy thrives in an alkaline environment, so I brought the right type of soil and water."

I smirked, "You've got everything figured out, huh?"

"Yeah, well I figured if she's gonna give me some ugly ivy to plant that I might as well make it the best."

It wasn't a bad logic to have, I thought to myself. But I asked, "You just couldn't resist looking it up," I said laughing and shaking my head. I would've looked it up too if Ellie hadn't stopped me.

"Nope. I mean, did she really expect us not to look it up? How did she expect us to grow this thing properly without knowing what it is?"

"I think she expected us to follow her directions step by step and wait and see what would happen."

"Well, I couldn't wait for that," she said, putting her hair up in a ponytail.

I smiled. "Do you like surprises Camila?"

"Not really."

"Yeah me neither," I agreed. I started preparing the pots with the soil. "There's just something in me that always feels like I gotta know what's next so I can prepare and know how to act and have enough money."

Her eyes widened. "Yes! Finally, someone gets it!"

"Yeah, I totally get it. But, I'm not sure if it's a good thing about me. It makes me want to control everything, how it happens, when it happens, it makes think I can be God," I said the words tumbling out of my mouth making me realize how uncomfortable and exposed I felt by my own confession.

I could read her face. She looked at me with her head cocked to one side like she was examining me and seeing if I was real. "Are you psychoanalyzing me?" she asked.

I shook my head slowly. "No, I think I'm psychoanalyzing me." I picked up the seeds. "And I think I know why Sister Titus gave you an ivy plant and not some mesmerizing flower or a fruit tree."

"Why?" she said, her voice filled with offense.

"Ivy is hard to control." It made me wonder just what type of plant she had given me. Too late to find out now, cause I had already buried mine beneath the earth.

She looked away. "So, she thinks I'm a control freak."

"Are you?" I asked quickly.

Her eyes defiantly met mine. "Maybe."

"You can't control everything."

"I know that, but what I can, I try to."

"Including your sister?" I fired back.

"What do you mean?"

"What does Valentina want to do? What does she dream about? Have you ever asked, or did you assume that your dreams were hers?"

The space between her eyebrows converged together. "Valé's never said she wanted to do anything, she always just wants to stay together."

"Maybe she just thinks that's what you want, and she doesn't want to disappoint you."

"Valé doesn't want to go to Georgetown?" her voice filled with confusion and hurt.

"I think that's a question you need to ask her."

Then I saw something I know all too well, not because I'm a counselor, but because I've experienced it. The fidgeting fingers, the avoidance, the shallow breaths: fear.

I know it made no sense to ask her if she was afraid. She would deny it. Instead I asked, "What are you afraid of?"

She was more honest than I was prepared for. More honest than I would've been. "Who am I going to be without Valentina?"

I held my arms out and drew her into an embrace. "You're gonna finally be Camila."

The next few days felt uncomfortable. I felt like I was now seeing myself again for the first time in a long time. Like a woman who has left her makeup on and takes it off to reveal a blemished face. I didn't like what I saw. I saw fear, I saw control issues, I saw low self-esteem, I saw a very broken me. I knew there was probably more to see because I had one more seed to help plant. Rachel's.

Something told me this might be the hardest one to plant.

6

Rachel and I grew up together. She and I were best friends. I covered her after she wet herself during field day because she was too scared to come down after doing the rope climb. I spilled water on my shorts too and I claimed that I accidentally spilled water just to buy time, so we could run home before anyone smelled something. She returned the favor when I had the stomach flu and got stuck in the bathroom in middle school. She told them she'd thrown a stink bomb in there. She got a week of detention for that and when we explained everything to the principal, both of us had detention for a week.

The principal was livid and so were our parents that we'd both lied. But, eventually they'd laughed it off and we both had stories to tell that had us laughing uncontrollably. We planned how we would leave Detroit and spend everyday on the beach here in Miami.

Rachel knew everything, she knew the songs I wrote, how I wanted to see Europe and Asia and just about everywhere in the world. She knew that I dreamed of wearing a ball gown at my wedding and of having three boys and one girl.

Rachel never wanted to be married. She'd always said that. She knew I didn't believe her, she knew that I knew it was only the pain of having an uncle repeatedly abuse her that made her afraid of men and afraid that marriage would turn into a lifelong prison of manipulation, abuse and control. She'd been there when I fell in love and thought I'd met the one. She was my only solace when it ended. Yet, I'd never told her everything. In fact, I didn't really tell her until everything had gone wrong.

But then, she'd met Keith when were in our last year of college together. He was so nice, and Rachel was so disinterested. She avoided him at all costs. I actually convinced her to give him a chance. I didn't want her past to kill her future. He was so patient though, he put up with all her lame excuses not to go out on a date. Her rude brushoffs and her apathetic behavior.

And it seemed like when she finally gave him a

chance she realized she wasn't waking into a prison, she was walking into a place she could call home. I'd always tease her about it and tell her that she'd been swirling all her life being best friends with me, and that I wasn't surprised that in Miami, she'd naturally find someone to swirl with for the rest of her life. When he proposed, I'm not sure who was happier, me or Rachel. We dove right into wedding planning. I was her maid of honor and we had the best time picking colors and dreaming up the whole big day. Until the day we went dress shopping. We'd done everything in one day, her bridal appointment and then the bridesmaid's bridal appointment. When Rachel came out in her dress, she'd looked like a dream. My dream. And I wiped away tears. But, I had a secret, those tears weren't for her, and I'd felt terribly guilty about that. Only I knew that the tears were for me. Only I knew that afterwards I had put on my maid of honor dress and stood there alone in that dressing room, in front of the vanity mirror, feeling dead inside, cause I was officially giving up hope.

So, from that moment on, I grew distant with her. I was still friendly and nice, but I stopped calling and texting as much, especially after she came back from her honeymoon. I found reasons to slide myself out of the picture, I told her that I wanted her to forge a bond with her husband. I told her that our friendship was meant to change after she got married. But, I didn't tell her the truth. That I was rotting with envy, like gangrene infecting every part of me. That the sight of her newfound happiness with Keith was enough to throw me into fits of self-pity. Now here I was, ringing the doorbell to her house, about to confront my once best friend and admit that I had to be the worst possible friend ever.

When she opened the door, I was greeted by her smile and her olive green eyes. "Hey, Autumn, it's nice to see you." She was wearing some old college sweats. Just like old times. Except that was six years ago.

"Hey, Rae."

"Come in."

I'd never been inside her house before. I'd always found some reason to decline the invitation, I'm swamped with work, I'm sick, I already agreed to another thing, blah, blah, blah.

I looked around at the cozy environment, the walls painted in neutral shades, the portraits of family, the wedding pictures and even one of the bridal party where my smile didn't quite reflect in my eyes.

My heart was thundering within me. I wanted to leave. I didn't want to plant this tree, or vine, or flower, or whatever it was.

I decided that small talk was best. I spotted a picture of Keith in his old Airforce uniform next to another guy with toffee colored skin that reminded me of Sister Blossom's. "Who's that?"

"Keith's cousin Matt."

"I don't remember him from the wedding," I said.

"He couldn't make it. He was actually supposed to be Keith's best man, don't you remember?"

I shook my head. "No, I don't."

"We haven't talked much since my wedding," she said.

I evaded her eyes. "No, we haven't."

"Did I do something to make you angry at me?" Rachel asked, her eyes even more green from the dark circles underneath them.

"What?"

"I've been wondering that for a long time. Did I do or say something? Because I want to make things right."

I shook my head and for the millionth time in just

two weeks I tried to hold back tears that I knew were coming. "No, you didn't do anything. It was me. It was all me." She deserved the truth.

She looked confused and I took a deep breath. "When you got engaged, I was so happy for you, and then I just wasn't as happy anymore, and that just snowballed into jealousy, cause I couldn't understand how you didn't want to be married and then all of a sudden you had everything that I'd always wanted. And I was jealous," I said shrugging. "I stayed away because seeing you happy made me unhappy. And I am the most selfish person for that," I said feeling like had to get out of here. "I don't think I should be here, I don't deserve to be here in your home. I should go," I said, making my way to the door and grabbing hold of the door knob.

"Wait."

I stopped, truly wanting to go. But, I knew I owed her the right to speak.

"Why didn't you just tell me before?"

I shrugged, and with the movement of my shoulders the tears fell down. "I didn't want you to worry about me, or for it to put a damper on anything. You were getting married. You were so happy."

She nodded. "Haven't I told you a million times that if you're hurting, then so am I?"

"That was supposed to be the happiest time of your life. I didn't want to add any sadness to it."

"But, I was sad. Cause you weren't there."

"I'm so sorry Rachel. Honestly, I really am. I'm sorry I've been avoiding you, I'm sorry about the babies," I said, fumbling with my hands as tears spilled over. "I'm so so sorry about the babies."

She wiped away a tear and put her hand in mine. "Yeah, well hopefully now, if I have one they'll have an aunt Autumn."

"You'd still want that?"

"I can't think of anything I'd want more," she said. "Besides who's gonna teach them how to climb a rope for field day?"

"Keith," I said laughing. "I'm too old to climb a rope now.

"Well, hopefully they won't be much of a rope climber."

"Well, you and Keith need to work cause I need my niece or nephew."

She laughed, "Yes, we will accomplish the will of the

Lord," she said reciting one of our old jokes.

"Be fruitful and multiply," I said and we both burst into peals of laughter heading outside to plant her seeds.

7

Let me tell you something about a seed and how it grows into a plant. You must first plant it and bury it. The environmental conditions have to be right. Cause if they're not, well then, you'll get a load of nothing. So, you gotta make sure it's buried deep enough or shallow, depending on what type of plant you're dealing with. The temperature has to be the right type of climate for that seed to germinate and the seed has to be watered. Now some seeds need more water than others and that's something you gotta be mindful of. You can't drown it, and you can't dehydrate it either.

Now when the seed is filled with water, something botanists call imbibtion, the water causes enzymes to form that will make the seed grow. A root will appear.

But mind you, you can't see this root because it's still underground. It's like the earth is keeping this huge secret from you, even though you're the seed planter. But at some point, the earth can't contain its secret just like a rumor that begins to spread, a shoot will burst forth from the ground, revealing that life has been there all along. And that's what happened with Camila, Valentina, and with Rachel.

Months after we'd planted, Valentina couldn't understand why Sister Blossom had asked her to practically starve her plants. She was told not to water them for weeks. I was afraid the poor plant would die. We couldn't see any life in the leaves. With that came the added anxiety for Valentina of telling her family about her decision to go to design school, as well as, waiting to hear if the school would give her a scholarship. She told Camila first, I'm sure Valentina was expecting Camila to spazz out, but God has a mysterious way of doing things. Maybe a week ago Camila would've told her that going to design school was ridiculous. But now, it wasn't so ridiculous. Camila joined forces with her sister to tell their parents. Their parents were nervous about them being apart, and get this, Camila forfeited Georgetown to go to Columbia to be closer to her sister.

And suddenly, Camila's ivy began to create a trellis up the side of the fence. I wasn't sure what to think of that, wasn't that ivy she planted a bad thing?

Sister Blossom came by their house the next day to see and to have a time of prayer with Camila and then with Valentina. They closed off the session watering Valentina's plants. The next day bright fuchsia blooms emerged, revealing itself to be bougainvillea.

Nowadays it seemed like everything dulled in comparison to anticipating the growth of these seeds. Work was just....work. School was about to be out, so most kids were in my office for test anxiety, anxiety about going away for college, anxiety, anxiety and more anxiety. I talked to them about coping, stress relieving techniques, and their life choices. But, I wished I could talk to them about more, about faith mostly. But, I couldn't.

Every morning I got up ready to write in my prayer journal and to get that text message from Sister Blossom with a scripture, a prayer or a thought for the day.

Even though all of us loved going to Harvest and singing the worship songs and hearing the word, it seem like we all craved those Wednesday meet ups with Sister Blossom where we shared the word with each other and prayed and believed for one more day that a miracle could happen.

Valentina called me the same day her bougainvillea bloomed. "Autumn, when you get off from work, can you come here please?"

"Is everything ok?"

"Yes, my flowers are here. I can't believe it. My flowers are here. You have to come and see them."

The twins lived about ten minutes away from where I worked. I didn't even need to come inside to see the blooms peeking out from the side of her fence. It was like she was waiting for me because she raced out of the house, her curls bouncing up and down with the rest of her as she jumped with excitement and said,

"Come in! Come in!"

I followed her inside her house and greeted Abuela and walked to the backyard with her.

I think we both stood there in silent awe of the beauty of the flowers.

"I finally get it now," she said.

"Get what?"

"I understand why I had to starve them."

"The bougainvillea?"

"Yes."

"Why?"

"Cause when you starve them they take in the water like their life depends on it. They bloom faster and brighter."

I chuckled. "That's actually interesting."

She shook her head. "No, that's actually me."

"What do you mean?"

She started laughing and shaking her head. "Oh, Sister T is good. She's good!"

"Am I missing something?"

"A year ago, Sister T asked me how did I feel? I told her fine, like I usually do. But, she asked again how do you feel? And I told her dry. That I felt like I was dried up and dead. I was just so...I was so caught up in living everyone else's dream and life that I felt like mine were dried up and dead. She told me that sometimes feeling dry isn't a bad thing. That sometimes God dries up our own resources so that we can return to him and that when we do we're more receptive and thankful for what he provides and so he'll pour out."

I didn't say anything. I didn't know what to say.

"I am the bougainvillea. She was trying to teach me something."

I still didn't know what to say. It's been four months and my plant hadn't even remotely emerged out of the ground even though I had been doing everything she told me to do. Now I was curious, what type of lesson Sister Blossom had in mind when she gave me my seed.

8

Another blind date. I don't know how I agreed to another blind date. Call it stupidity, desperation or hopeless romanticism, but when a coworker kept insisting I go out on a date with her brother, I agreed. Why did I agree? It was summer break, I could've easily just avoided her calls. I felt like banging my head against the wall.

"Why are you being so negative?" Ellie asked as she sat on my couch with her laptop as I stood in front of the mirror applying lipstick and adjusting my curled hair. "It could be great you know. What if he's the sweetest guy, loves Jesus, and is handsome?" Ellie always stayed at my house the night I had a date. I did it for two reasons. I could always go home and talk about the date with her.

Plus, her being home made sure that I got home and didn't bring anyone else home either.

I rolled my eyes. "Just be on the lookout for the code word I'm gonna send you after you send me the check-up text. All you have to do is ask what flavor ice cream should you pick up. The date starts at seven, so you can send it around 7:45. I should know by then if he's a lunatic." He and I had texted back and forth and talk once on the phone. He seemed ok, but you can never be so sure.

"Yeah, yeah, yeah, cookies and crème if it's going good."

"And if it's going bad?" I said quizzing her.

She rolled her eyes. "Rum raisin."

"Thank you." I pursed my lips. "Do you think that this could really be it?"

She smiled. "Yeah, I think so. You know me, I try and stay hopeful."

"Thanks, El." I took a deep breath and picked up my purse and keys. "How do I look?" I said looking down at my deep purple dress. "Like you're ready to slay," she said snapping her fingers.

I shook my head and laughed. "You're so dumb."

"Nervous?" she asked me.

"Always."

If I thought I was nervous then, then I must've been a wreck as I waited at the restaurant for 15 minutes. No sign of him. 7:30 came and my nervousness turned to concern. I texted him, to check where he was and by 7:40 the text came back with one simple reply. "Not going to be there tonight." There was no call, there was no apology or explanation. I wanted to feel angry, but instead I felt my face grow warm and tears pool around my eyes. The waitress came back, "Any word from him?" and now I really felt like I was gonna cry.

"He's not coming," I said in a monotone voice.

Her eyes widened before she said, "Jerk."

I nodded and got up to leave.

"Hey, I mean we can at least give you a drink on the house."

"No, thanks," I said, walking briskly to my car, wondering how many people had seen me pathetically sitting there for 40 minutes alone, dressed up, looking through the menu, only to leave. The same biting thoughts came back that he didn't want to come because he probably thought I was some loser that couldn't get a date otherwise, or that he had a girlfriend already, or that he thought I was ugly. My phone buzzed, and I saw Ellie's text.

What flavor ice cream should I pick up?

I got to my car, opened the door and sat inside finally letting the tears roll down as I texted her back.

Rum raisin.

9

I was usually the happiest in the summer, as a school counselor I was officially on break and I could just sleep in and travel. Today, I was at the beach in Biscayne with Ellie and Rachel. Ellie had a few days off before she had to head back to the airport for non-stop flights for the next couple weeks. Rachel, Ellie and I laid down on our beach towels and I let the warm sun and the sound of the waves soothe me as I started to drift off.

"So how did that blind date go?" Rachel asked me.

"Ughhhhhh," I groaned. "I don't want to talk about it." I turned my face away from them, trying to fall asleep again.

"That bad?" she said.

"Worse than rum raisin ice cream," Ellie said.

"Hey, I like rum raisin," Rachel said.

Ellie laughed. "Right now, the way things are looking for Autumn and I, we probably need some rum to drown our sorrows."

"You better not," Rachel said.

"I'm kidding."

Only I knew that Ellie was not. Ellie was usually out of town, she worked as a flight attendant and I was grateful for the times, she would give me a pass, so I could travel. She was gone so often that someone often had to stop at her place, just to make sure things were ok. Sometimes Ellie was so stressed out about her bills that she called me panicked.

Her load was easier when her sister was still remotely stable and working, but as her addiction worsened she lost her job as a makeup artist. Ellie struggled not to be an enabler most times. Whenever Emmy would come home begging for more cash or a place to crash, Ellie would let her, and then something would go missing. Ellie would kick her out and then the cycle would repeat because Ellie carried around the guilt of first introducing her sister to prescription painkillers. Em had started getting migraines, like debilitating ones. They'd tried everything, but sometimes Em was doubled over in pain. So, one day, Ellie suggested that Em take some painkillers Ellie had from an old operation. It worked. Em was able to function, but not able to stop taking the pills. Even when the pills ran out, Em found someone selling pills, then eventually the pills weren't enough and Em started shooting up. Her first time she almost died from an overdose. Ellie always goes back to the day when she gave her that first pill and that's why she always enabled her.

But, one day Ellie got adamant about taking the tough love route and cut Emmy off of everything. When she found out that Emmy had gotten an abortion after getting pregnant from her dealer, Ellie was distraught. Not even I could console her. The only person that seemed able to do anything was Sister Blossom. I don't know what she said or did, but I stood on the inside of the house, watching them outside in the backyard, talking by the place where Ellie had planted her seeds, Sister Blossom rubbing her back and speaking while Ellie's tears seemed to water the ground.

"Eww, what's that smell?" Rachel said, snapping me back to the present time.

"What smell?" Ellie said.

"The ocean smells so...salty."

I turned back over and laughed. "What do you expect it to smell like?"

"I don't know. It doesn't smell super strong?"

"No," I drawled.

"I think I ate something weird guys, cause I feel sick to my stomach."

Ellie chimed in again, "I told you not to eat that sushi and then ice cream. Raw fish and ice cream should never be combined."

Rachel moaned and then got up and rushed to the nearest trashcan, vomiting everything she'd eaten.

Ellie and I took Rachel to the hospital after she'd vomited twice in the car ride to her house. Food poisoning was the worst. Ellie offered to stay with her at the hospital until Keith came while I raced to her house to get some things for her. I followed her instructions and got some sweats and toiletries when I spotted something outside of her window. Dots of white spread over her backyard. My phone rang, and it was Rachel.

"Hey, I got the bag, I should be heading to you soon," I said, before she interrupted me.

"I'm not sick."

"What do you mean you're not sick?"

"I'm pregnant," she said, her voice shaking with awe, excitement, and tears mixed into one.

"What?" I whispered.

I got the overnight bag I packed for her and headed to the backyard and walked over to the patch I had seen. I covered my mouth in shock that the white dots I had seen weren't white dots, Rachel's backyard was now filled with baby's breath.

Sunday, I picked up Sister Blossom as usual. Her outfits weren't getting any better. Today she had on a yellow skirt suit with those white stockings and white shoes. She entered and started her usual line of questioning, although since our planting time, her questions didn't bother me as much anymore.

"What's the plans for your break?"

"Rest," I said. "I may take a short trip if Ellie can get me a pass."

"Sounds fun, anywhere in particular you're planning to go?"

"I was just thinking of going to this songwriting workshop in New York. I'm not sure though, I mean I'm not a professional or anything and-"

"What's the problem? Go."

I shook my head. "I'm still thinking about it."

"Mmmmm hmmm."

"Sister Blossom, I know when we started this we said that we would treat these seeds like they were our literal miracles and I got it. But, I thought this would be symbolic. But, Rachel's seeds bloomed right when she found out she was pregnant and right after Valé's bloomed, she got the scholarship to Parsons. I'm not a believer in magic nor in coincidences, but-"

She cut to the chase. "Are you asking me if these seeds are directly linked to your miracle?"

"Yes."

"Depends on your faith."

"How is that possible?" I murmured. "That's not possible."

"Faith makes anything possible."

"But there's a natural order to things. Things have to make sense. This just doesn't make sense."

"Then my dear, you don't understand faith."

"I'm honestly trying to. Right now, I'm seeing everyone's seeds growing, except mine."

She smiled. "Can you see beneath the soil?"

"No."

"So why do you assume your seed is dead?"

I was about to say because I can't see any sprouts, but I decided against it. That would confirm my faithlessness.

"There is a mystery beneath the earth in the same way Rachel will be experiencing a mystery inside of her. Before you all had your fancy gadgets, no one had any clue what their baby looked like or if it was a girl or boy."

"But they could see it growing"

"Yes, they can, but so can you."

"I told you, nothing has happened, and I've done exactly what you told me to do every day."

"With faith you would be able to see."

"You're speaking in riddles."

She smiled. "The problem is that you care too much about what is happening for others. Your comparison leads to anxiety and then you just try to control everything. You can't control time nor what others do."

"You think I need to not care?"

"I didn't say that. If you don't get what you want, will you still be faithful to God?"

My first instinct was to say yes, but I knew that there were times that I complained against God, times I feigned sickness, so I didn't have to serve, but I was really just sick from disappointment or anxiety. "I'm not sure if I would. I would want to, but sometimes my emotions get the best of me."

"God will not give you anything to replace him."

"I don't want to replace God."

"What do you think happens when you think about the gift more than the giver?"

She shut me up and her words lodged in my chest like an arrow. So, believe it or not, that started my sabbatical. For six months I didn't look for a date, I didn't accept a date or a blind date. I took my time once again learning who God was. Focusing on him and reading his word. I smashed the idol that I once had, and I allowed God to replace it with something else.

Contentment.

I still saw no movement from my seed. The ground was now covered back in grasses, but no plant emerged. I asked Sister Blossom several times if this was normal, if there was a chance that my plant had died beneath the soil, but she assured me everything was ok. Almost a year after the planting, I was looking back and smiling now that I had joyfully watched Camila and Valentina graduate and I saw Rachel's stomach grow into the giant beach ball that it is now. I saw her joy at finding out that it wasn't just one child, but two. Two boys. A double portion. Keith had come back from his flight and had gone with her to the ultrasound. Both of them facetimed me later in fits of laughter that turned to tears of gratitude. Two boys, look at God.

But, we're humans, you know, and one minute we know that only God can do it, and in the next we think it's up to us.

"Autumn what if they die?" Rachel said to me, her eyes red rimmed as she sat crumpled on the floor of their nursery. She was 28 weeks today, no complications, none of the painful shots she used to do in the past. It was a miracle. She was a walking miracle with two babies inside of her that God had securely placed in there. I wondered if God spoke to them in her womb and how with birth they would have to relearn how to hear his voice once again. Just like we all had to.

It's hard to hear him with the deafening sound of fear ringing in your ears. Sometimes it sounds like the thumping of your heart, sometimes it's in the voice of others from long ago. It didn't matter, it beckoned to us differently and we all fought like mad to ignore it. And sometimes we failed.

She had been in this nursery many times, hoping, dreaming, only to have those dream die weeks later.

"They're not going to die," I said with finality.

"That's what Keith said every time. I'm not even sure if he believed it when he said it. I pray and I pray and I can't shake this fear. If God let the others die, how do I know they won't either?"

I nodded. I didn't know what to say, every thought that could come to mind didn't seem like a good one. I could quote scriptures, I could tell her that doubt canceled out any miracles. However, she nor Keith needed that kind of guilt or those words. All I did was rest my head on her shoulder and place a hand on her stomach.

"They're here with you and so am I."

She took a breath and put her hand over mine and I realized maybe that's all she needed to know in that moment.

When Keith came back from his piloting route, Rachel was now busy and so I was alone, waiting for Ellie to come home from doing her flight attendant route. I don't even remember which country she was supposed to be in right now. I lost track sometimes because of how often she traveled.

When I heard a key going into my front door as I was reading, I got excited. The only person with a key was Ellie. The door opened, and she said, "What's up?! I'm back!" She was still wearing her flight attendant uniform, scarf still in place.

I laughed loudly. "Hey what's up? Where are you coming back from?"

She plopped down on the couch next to me. "Paris." She sighed loudly. "I told you that you could've come this time."

"I don't remember you asking, but Paris? Nope, I think I'm good."

"How would you know? You've never been there."

I tapped my fingers against the book I was holding. "I have been to Paris, years ago. Not really interested in going back."

"Why? I like Paris."

"There's nothing wrong with the city El. I just have bad memories of there."

"Must be some really bad memories, considering that this is the first I've ever known that you even stepped foot on European soil."

I rolled my eyes and got up to get some of the snickerdoodle cookies I had. "Want some?" I asked Ellie.

"Yeah," she said reaching for some and taking a few out the box. "So, are you gonna tell me what happened in Paris?"

I rolled my eyes again. "I went there to elope," I said matter of factly.

Ellie burst into laughter. "Autumn, come on! Stop playing with me!"

I gave a small smile. "Nah, I just had a bad experience. Someone was supposed to fly with me there and bailed and I got stuck in Paris for a week by myself," I said taking back refuge in half truths.

Ellie shook her head in amusement. "That sucks. Well, you should've just met you a Pierre or an Antoine."

I laughed. "Yeah, I need a Frenchman who speaks no English. That way I don't have to worry about saying anything stupid."

Ellie laughed. "You're so dumb," she said, taking a bite of the cookie. "No, you need someone who only speaks Spanish. They can't understand what you're saying, but you understand them."

"You're right. I didn't take those six years of Spanish for nothing." I took my last bite of the cookie. "Any word from Em yet?"

She looked out the window and shook her head. "Nope. I stopped paying her phone bill. She's only been using it to call her dealer." Ellie shrugged. "She's probably just doing her thing."

"She might be in rehab for all you know," I said.

"You're right," she said. "You know, it's funny how you can always think the best for someone else, but not for you," she scolded.

"Gosh, I have everyone on my case lately."

"We only do it because we care."

"Yes, I'm feeling the love," I said sarcastically. "Right now, I'm not feeling the love from my crew nor from that plant outside."

Ellie chuckled and pulled the curtains aside to look outside. "Yeah, that plant seems like it's a bit stubborn. Just like its planter. I think Sister Blossom picked the perfect plant for you Autumn."

Well, Ellie was tough on me, but Camila was a bit easier on my ego. Camila and I texted back and forth every day. She was doing well at Columbia. I called her one day as I headed home from work on a cool December day.

"Hey, how are you? How's school?"

"It's been good. I love the classes and the city and everything Autumn. I don't know why I thought about going anywhere else. Can you believe we're at the end of our first semester of college?"

"I can't!" I said laughing. "God's plans are better than ours, most times we just don't understand it."

"Yeah, Valé and I met up at least twice a week and go somewhere to eat or just hang out. Even in the cold or snow, we always meet up."

"That's awesome."

"She's so happy. I've never seen my sister like this. It's like she's finally free."

"Yes, I think she is."

"All of us held her back for too long. I never even realized how my own jealousy held her back, you know."

"Jealousy?"

"Yes, I saw my sister as this…" she sighed. "I don't know for some reason I thought she was better and so I coped by competing. I drove her down with my attitude and words to stay on top. And I was fighting my own sister. My own mirror image. I realize maybe the whole time I was really fighting myself."

I sat there in traffic mulling over her words.

"Are you there?" she asked.

"Yeah, I'm here," I said. "How did you figure all of this out?"

"When Sister T gave me the bag of seeds, it had a scripture on a small piece of paper. I still have it here in my room, hold up, let me get it." There was a shuffling and then she came back. "It was Proverbs 14:30. 'A sound heart is the life of the flesh: but envy the rottenness of the bones.'"

"But your plant was the first to grow. It grew after you helped Valentina."

"I did help her. That didn't mean I wasn't jealous."

I guess you can never tell someone's heart, even when their actions seem pure. Is that why she was given ivy? A green plant that grew out of control that would break up the mortar of your home if it wasn't controlled?

She continued, "I was mad when I saw it. Really mad. But, I kept it and it kept bothering me. And I thought, to myself why did she give me a plant I didn't want and when I realized that Valé had a bougainvilla I wondered why she'd given her a pretty plant and not me. My ivy was ruining every pot it had been put in. It clicked then. I just knew, I knew the scripture was for me. The ivy was for me. I uprooted it and threw it out a little before I left for New York."

"You dumped your plant? Why didn't you tell me? Does Sister Blossom know that you got rid of it?"

"Yeah, she does. I love her, but she's different. She sat down and thought of all of this. She was hoping I'd get the message and throw it out. When I did, she had another seed ready for me."

"She gave you a new seed?"

"Yeah.

"And you planted it?" I asked.

"Yeah, I did. I didn't even check to see what it was this time. She put a new scripture in my bag this time. Isaiah 43:18-19, But the Lord says 'do not cling to the events of the past or dwell on what happened long ago. Watch for the new thing I am going to do. It is happening already- you can see it now! I will make a road through the wilderness and give you streams of water there.'"

"What do you think it means?" I asked.

"She told me to water this seed regularly, but not to drown it. I'm not one hundred percent sure what it all means for me specifically. But, now I feel new, I am new and I'm starting a new journey, knowing myself, loving myself, loving God and that feels refreshing. I found a church up here, and so has Valé. I never knew my soul was thirsty until now."

"Yeah, I see what you mean." I wish I could see myself more clearly too. Sometimes, I wonder if I ever will and sometimes I wonder if I truly want to see. Maybe ignorance will be bliss.

It's been a year and a month since the planting. Still nothing out of the ground. At this point, I only water it because if I don't everyone will get on my case. I'm not sure what type of seeds I was given but those seeds are probably defunct for all I know. What type of plant takes this long to come out of the ground? So, I looked it up, and guess what I saw? A bunch of giant trees like cedar or oaks that take hundreds of years to grow…Sister Blossom must've really lost it giving me this. I would never get to see this plant. Only my great, great, great grandkids would get to enjoy these trees and that was if I had any the way my love life looked.

Honestly, the more I thought about it, the madder I got. Why was she trying me like this? Even Ellie's had now grown into a small vine coming out of the ground that none of us could identify. Sister Blossom had come by and helped her to twine the vines together. She said they were meant to grow together and strengthen each other. At this point I think both me and Ellie were fed up with this process, me even more so.

Sister Blossom had asked me to come by and help her cook dinner for Rachel, Ellie and I. I went over and as she worked on the baked mac and cheese, I started peeling the potatoes.

"Did you give me a cedar tree?" I asked.

"What?" she asked, her back turned to me as she placed the tray in the oven.

"Did you give me a cedar tree?" I repeated.

"Now, why would you ask a question like that?" she still hadn't turned to face me.

"Because I need to know. It's been over a year and everyone's plant has grown but mine, so either my plant is dead or it's something that's gonna take forever to grow."

She chuckled and finally turned to me. "Do you need to know everything?"

"Not everything."

"Just enough so you can control it."

Ok, so here we went again, where the plant talk now spilled over into a discussion about my life. "Is it wrong for me to not want to feel like my life is out of control?"

"Your life will always be out of control if you're the one trying to control it."

"How do I give control to someone else? It's my life. I have to live it. I have to know what's around the bend. I have to know if something is going to pop out around the corner and hurt me."

She nodded. "Who hurt you?"

"What?" I said, putting down the knife I was using to peel. "No one has hurt me."

"It's ok, you can tell me."

"Sister Blossom right now you're hurting me by giving me this stupid tree that won't grow for 200 years. That's what's hurting me."

"I'm sorry you feel that way, now who else?"

"We're not doing this right now," I said. "I respect you, you're old enough to be my grandma and I don't want to have an argument."

"We don't have to. What made you feel out of control?"

A flashback came to me. An attendant asking me if I was ready to board. "Are you still going to wait?" he had asked me. His voice had been gravelly. Hoarse. Raspy.

"I was supposed to get married," I said. I wasn't sure she would understand what I meant.

"I had everything planned. We were gonna elope to Paris. I had bought the tickets. I had this lace dress. I had gotten a deal on it. I didn't tell anyone, not even Rachel. I was still in college. I was only 20. I didn't tell her until everything had gone bad."

"What happened?" she asked.

"He never showed up. I waited until everyone boarded our flight. He never showed up. I knew he wasn't coming, but some part of me was still hoping. I told myself he was stuck somewhere with no signal and that's why he wasn't answering his phone. So, I got on the flight. I ended up spending the whole week in Paris alone."

"What did your fiancé say?"

I gave a hardened smile and shook my head. "My fiancé...." The words tasted like bile coming out of my mouth. "He told me there was no way he would actually marry me. The proposal was basically a shut up ring. He thought that if he proposed, then he could move forward physically in the relationship. He didn't think I'd *actually* require marriage."

I took a breath and wiped at the tears I hadn't realized and streamed down my face and sniffled. "The next week he was with someone new. My dumb self decided that I needed closure. As if, the whole Paris thing and the girl wasn't enough. It was like I was hoping that he didn't mean those things he had said. He told me that he had never been happy with me and never would be because his new girl was, and I quote, everything I wasn't: pretty and down for whatever."

I took a deep breath and smoothed back my hair. "Come on, Autumn, did you really think I'd stick around for long when you wouldn't let me hit?" I felt the tears flowing back down again. "I guess I should've thanked God for sending that false report so that I would really know what was in that guy's heart. But, I was mad. Mad at God and even more mad at him."

"Why were you mad at God?"

I rubbed my eyes and looked away. "I've always heard that if God takes something away it's because he has something better for you. But, not for me. I waited, and I waited, and nothing came."

"Perhaps he didn't want you to wait for another man. Perhaps he wanted you to wait for him."

"Yes. Perhaps," I said shortly.

"Do you know how much God loves you?"

I snorted. "Yes."

"Do you really?"

"Died on a cross to save me, I'd have to think twice about taking a bullet for someone I knew much less someone who would repeatedly sin against me."

"You say these words with your mouth, but I'm not sure your heart understands them."

I leaned forward, arms extended on the counter. "What do you want from me Sister Blossom? I feel like you've brought me through a year of this bizarre therapy and I've been open. I have. I've been trying to do everything you've asked. But all you do is ask questions and you give me no solution. I want an answer!" I said slamming my fist against the counter. "All I've ever asked is for a yes or no." I said, my voice trembling with fury. "At this point I don't even care if it's a yes or no. But all I get is wait and see. All I get is try harder, do this one more thing to grow more and I do it and it's never enough. It's never enough! I'm never enough!"

The last words escaped my mouth in a rush of anger before I could pull them back. Again, I felt the same feeling of exposure, I wanted to go back and clothe myself behind my stony exterior, but I stood there, my mouth agape, thinking about what I had just said.

"Who told you that lie?" she asked sternly. It was the first time she'd ever addressed me this way, even when I had shown annoyance and even disrespect, she'd never been angry, until now.

"He did."

"And you believed him."

I nodded.

I felt the need to explain. "He was never really nice to me. Only when he wanted something, and I was always trying so hard to be everything he wanted me to be and he threw me away. I did my best, I loved him so much and he threw me away. Then I got older and I realized I couldn't love him the way I thought I did. I was so blind that I couldn't see him for who he really was, because he wasn't hiding it. I was ignoring it. I felt stupid. But, I can't get his words out of my head and every time I try with another guy they're never interested, they always want someone else. Never me."

"Now how did you expect to hear God's voice when all you've been listening to is lies?"

The doorbell rang. Ellie and Rachel were here, and I went back to making mashed potatoes, feeling extremely tired, but again feeling like I could breathe easier.

10

Twice the blessing, twice the fun, two miracles instead of one, I read on the giant easel as I walked into Rachel's baby shower. I'd offered to help with the set up and the planning, but Rachel insisted that I relax and just enjoy the shower.

"You're always planning stuff. Don't you just miss being a part of the party?" she said.

No, I didn't miss being a part of the party. I wanted to feel useful, I wanted to do something. But, I respected Rachel's wishes and let her family act as hosts. We laughed uproariously as we played the different games and I smiled as I saw the blending of two families, black and white, and friends of all races and nationalities all excited to celebrate the miracle that had happened and the miracle to come. It was a glimpse of heaven.

"Autumn!"

The sound of my name brought me out of my trance and I looked up to see them beckoning me to play one of the games.

I shook my head nervously and the whole party started chanting my name, telling me to go. I stood up and made my way to the center of the floor where the two other lucky ladies stood.

"So, we're gonna blind fold you ladies and you're going to stand behind a gentleman and feed him baby food," Rachel's sister Melanie said.

I laughed. "Well, I sure hope it's not green peas."

"Actually, it's butternut squash, which I'm not sure will be much better," I heard a deep voice behind me and I turned around to see a conveniently handsome guy. Where had I seen him before? He towered over me, which wasn't a difficult feat considering most kids by age twelve were taller than me.

"They say you're my partner," he said. "I'm Matt. Keith's cousin."

Then I remembered. He was the guy from the picture in Rachel's house. I almost wanted to give a bitter laugh. Of course, this would happen to me. Cute guy, incredibly awkward moment to follow as I most likely will ruin his clothes or make him throw up.

"Hey Matt, I'm-

"Autumn," he said smiling. "Yeah, the crowd was chanting it pretty well."

I smiled in spite of my embarrassment or maybe because of it. I caught a glimpse of Ellie making "oh la la" faces to make me laugh. I suddenly felt self-conscious, did my hair look alright? Was this navy maxi dress even cute?

"Ok, here's the rules guys," Melanie started to explain before telling us that the women couldn't peek under their blind fold and the men couldn't touch our hands, only guide us through words.

When they said to start, I tried using one hand to feel his face to see where his mouth would be and then I realized just how awkward that felt so I just tried to put the spoon at his mouth. I don't think I was doing such a great job considering he kept saying, "Autumn!" in between laughing at my pathetic attempts. Even I was laughing, half from embarrassment, half from amusement.

Well… let's just say when I lifted my blindfold, there

was orange mush all over Matt's mouth, chin, cheeks and even a splatter on his eyebrow. Not to mention the orange splatter on his shirt and pants. I covered my mouth in shock.

I moved my hands back to my sides. "I am sooooooo sorry," I said, wide-eyed.

He laughed. "It's cool."

"Are you sure? I could buy you a new shirt. I could-"

He laughed again. "Autumn, I have a washing machine. I promise you, it's cool."

I nodded. "Ok, thanks." I walked off and went back to sit in front of Ellie.

"That was so embarrassing," I said, plopping down on the chair.

Ellie cleared her throat. "Well, I don't think you did so bad, because he's looking at you."

"What?" I whispered.

"He's coming over here," she whispered quickly, before Matt pulled a seat next to me. Even though his hair was cut low I could see that he had curly hair.

"Is it ok if I sit here?" he asked.

"Yeah, sure," Ellie said enthusiastically, and he took a seat.

"Did you come for me to pay your cleaning tab?" I said sarcastically jabbing him and realizing he smelled really good in spite of having baby food all over him.

"Awww, Autumn ya gotta forgive yourself," he joked. "Hey, I'm Matt, Keith's cousin," he said extending his hand out to Ellie. He had dimples. I liked dimples. *Yeah, yeah, Autumn. Dimples, nice smile, muscles, good style. He's either just like all the rest or totally uninterested in you.*

Ellie nodded and smiled. I rolled my eyes, knowing that she was about to pull her usual act whenever I was around a guy. I couldn't get her to stop socializing until I was with a guy and then she made me do all the work while she pretended to be mute.

"I didn't see you at their wedding, I thought I met everyone there," I said trying to make small talk. I mean, I knew why he wasn't there. I couldn't tell him that. I'd look like a stalker.

"Oh, yeah, I'm in the Air Force. I couldn't get the release to come. I was pretty bummed about that. I'm actually very bummed that tomorrow I head back out."

"So, the Air Force runs in the family?"

"Yeah, definitely. My dad, Keith's dad, and us. Just hoping to make this my last tour and then it's home to find some piloting work."

"Tired of the military life?" Ellie asked.

"Yeah, I guess, you get older and you want to settle down and be like Keith and Rachel and have a couple of these parties."

"Ahhh I see, Autumn weren't you saying the same thing the other day?" Ellie asked.

If looks could cut, then Ellie would've been sliced and diced. "I don't know, I say a lot of things."

"Ahh, Ellie, quit bugging Autumn," Matt said.

"Yes, Ellie, quit bugging me," I said straightforwardly.

"So, let me guess, everyone is trying to play matchmaker?" he asked.

"Story of my life."

"Yeah, our partnership was probably preplanned."

"I wouldn't put it past Rachel," I said as I smiled.

"And I wouldn't put it past Keith. He did this when we were teenagers at church back in California. Even when we went to separate colleges. He kept trying to get me to move to Miami with him by telling me he had some great girl for me to meet."

"Yup," I said, trying to figure out what to say next to

not make the conversation awkward. I for sure wasn't going to tell him about how often one of my friends or these church ladies tried to set me up with someone. I decided to switch topics. "You said this'll probably be your last tour. But you probably have some exciting places to visit. So, what's next for you?"

He thought for a bit. "Dinner, with you tonight, if that's ok, then it's back to Italy on base there."

My throat got dry and Ellie kicked me underneath the table and I turned to face him still unsure what to say. I know what I was thinking: *Yes, but no, because you'll probably be like all the others.*

"Yes. That's more than ok."

But those words didn't come from me. They came from Ellie.

"Well, I've got Ellie's blessing. But is that ok with you Autumn?" he asked.

I nodded. "Yes. That'd be nice."

He smiled genuinely. Like he was actually excited, while I was wondering what did I just set myself up for?

"Well, you know what," he said, looking at his watch. "It's already after five o' clock, I'm gonna head home and clean up. Yeah, I'm not going anywhere covered in butternut squash."

"Thank God it wasn't green peas," I muttered.

He smiled and asked for my number and address and told he would come and get me around 8:00, and then he was gone. When he left, I sat there my mouth open, trying to figure out what just happened. "Why did I just agree to go out on a date?"

"Because he's this super cute, sweet guy, who Rachel and Keith have worked really hard to get in contact with you."

"What?" I said, my head snapping up to look at Ellie. "They what?"

I turned around and saw Rachel and Keith looking at me, smiling and laughing in my direction. I glared back at them and they walked over.

"He asked you out, right?" Keith said.

"You did this?" I asked.

"Yes, I did," he said. Rachel nudged him. "Well, we did this. This has been a long time coming."

What did he mean by that? I didn't bother to ask him. "Keith, love you, but this is a lot of pressure, what if I think your cousin doesn't end up liking me or what if I don't like him?"

"Not happening," Keith said. "This has been well thought out. Rachel wanted to do this from the time of the wedding."

Rachel chimed in. "Yeah, when I met Keith's family out in Cali I really thought Matt would be a good fit, but then he couldn't make it out for the wedding, so when I heard he was coming to the shower, I was so excited."

I was annoyed with them, but they did this to be sweet. Plus, I mean I've had people straight up disrespect me with the type of people they picked out for me. Matt was a really nice, good looking guy. But did he-

Rachel touched my shoulder. "He's the real deal. Trust me. The man prays and studies more than me," she said.

I rolled my eyes and laughed. "You really did your homework, didn't you?"

Ellie chimed in. "Autumn stop your foolishness, so we can get home and get you ready."

"I can't stand all of you," I said. "I'm only being nice because you're pregnant Rachel. Keith and Ellie, you guys are still on my hit list."

Keith laughed. "The girl who can't open a jar by herself is threatening all of us."

I stuck my tongue out him and smiled. My friends were the most nosy, meddling bunch and I loved them. Now, what was I going to wear to this thing?

Matthias Anderson. He hated his name. Matthias was too weird to tell people. Matt made everyone think he was white.

We sat across from each other at a rooftop restaurant in downtown Miami. I'd never been here before. Shoot, I'd never been to a rooftop restaurant in Miami. It was night time and the skyline was lit up. I could hear the sound of the water of Biscayne Bay. The wind was strong, but thankfully not whipping my hair and this dress all over the place.

Ellie basically took over my outfit selection. She picked out this airy floral print long sleeved dress that stopped a bit before my knee, complete with drop earrings and wedge heels. She wanted me to wear makeup. I refused. I told her, he's already seen my natural face at the shower, it won't kill him to see it again. I put on some tinted lip balm and called it a day. He was wearing a white button down short sleeved shirt with a pair of jeans.

I was so nervous that I ordered a salad. I never order a salad. But, I didn't want to order a burger on a date. I wasn't trying to look like I eat nothing. I just didn't want to look sloppy, because I had ketchup on the side of my mouth or something.

"You know, you can eat whatever you want, right?" he said. "Judgement free zone."

I laughed. "How did you know I didn't want a salad?"

"Cause I saw the way you were tearing into those chicken wings at the shower," he said.

I opened my mouth in shock. "Oh, my goodness!"

We both laughed as I covered my face. I did change my order though. Well, I added some fries to the order. I must admit, after the first twenty minutes at dinner I realized Matt made me feel comfortable. I was laughing more, talking about life in Detroit.

"I mean I'm a mixed kid, Dad is American and Mom is Mexican. I'm a military brat, my parents eventually settled down in Oakland and I'm walking around telling people my name is Matt," he said. "But, it grew on me. Even Matthias. I won't walk around telling people to call me that, but it's not so bad."

"With that name, I expect you to walk around with Jesus sandals," I said as we laughed.

"Gee, thanks!" he said as he laughed and wiped his mouth with a napkin. "So, what's next for you?" he asked.

I toyed with the stem of the water goblet. "I don't know, for the first time in my life, I don't know."

"Always had your life all planned out, huh?"

"Always."

"What was supposed to happen?"

I chuckled. I couldn't tell him that. No guy wanted the truth on a first date, they wanted sugar coated lies. "Do you really want to know?"

"Yes. I do."

He would leave anyways. He had the perfect excuse, he was going back to Italy tomorrow. Might as well tell the truth.

"I wanted to get married and travel everywhere, India, Thailand, Kenya, Sweden, just anywhere spreading the gospel, singing songs, then have a few kids. It's pretty dumb. Not realistic."

He didn't respond to my last comments. "How

many?"

"Three. Two boys. One girl."

"Names?" He asked with genuine interest or maybe I just thought it was genuine interest.

"Not Matthias." I said, and we both dissolved into laughter.

"Ok, so I agree a Matthias Jr, wouldn't be the best idea," he conceded, taking a sip of his water.

"Matthias Jr.? First date and you're already naming our children?"

He put his glass down. "Oh, come on, you probably already had them planned Autumn, or you wouldn't be here."

Again, my jaw naturally dropped and then I smirked and shook my head. "You think you're clever. Hasn't anyone told you this is really taboo conversation for a first date?" I wondered if Rachel and Keith put him up to this.

"It is, and I wouldn't be having this conversation with anyone else. I just know that a woman like you has your wedding planned and your kids names," he said leaning back.

"Did Rachel and Keith put you up to this?"

"Nope. But, I'm guessing I'm right."

"It's not true."

"No?"

"I'm still working on the middle names and figuring out how everything will fit in the orchard."

I put my hand over my face in embarrassment as we both laughed heartedly again.

"The orchard?" he asked confused.

"My parents own an orchard in Michigan. It's been passed down for generations. I always wanted to get married there." I sipped from my glass nervously.

"What's wrong?" he asked.

"I don't know why I just told you that. I don't think I've told anyone that."

He looked surprised. "Well, then I'm honored. I won't tell anyone," he said genuinely.

I could feel myself wrestling with my emotions. We don't need promises between us, you're leaving and I'm not getting my hopes up. I decided to cut to the chase.

"Look Matt, I'm a Christian. Like the type that won't sleep with you until I'm married. I go to church every week, I read my bible every day, I'll probably annoy you with my singing, and I use ten percent of my income and give it to God."

"Word?" he said slowly. "Gosh… I mean I don't know if I can be down with the singing. Can we throw some beat boxing in there too?"

I stared at him.

He smiled. "Was that supposed to scare me?" he asked. "Cause all of that sounded pretty dope to me. But, I'm still curious to know these kids' names since you're hating on mine so heavy."

I didn't know what to say really. That usually turned everyone away. I took a deep breath.

"Wait, what is happening?" I said incredulously.

"You're trying to self- sabotage this date, by thinking that telling me you're a Christian would do the trick, and I'm basically telling you I wouldn't be here if I didn't think you were. So, unless you got something really scary to tell me, you can continue with giving me those baby names."

I couldn't hide my smile. "Joshua, Caleb, and Mary."

"Mary?" he asked. "You lost me at that one," he said.

"They're all names of people with great faith," I said.

He nodded. "I get it, it's kind of ironic you'd pick those names, yet you're doubting if God can do that for you."

"I didn't say he couldn't. I don't know if he will."

"What makes you think he won't?"

I shrugged. "Maybe God has a different plan."

He leaned back. "Maybe he does, but, that doesn't mean his plan isn't similar to yours. I just think God has a different way of doing it."

"Delight yourself in the Lord, right?"

"Yes!" he said. "Yes."

"Done that, it didn't work."

He raised an eyebrow. "If you really did it, we wouldn't be having this conversation."

I shrugged. "I asked if you really wanted to know."

"You did ask, and I still want to know."

Why did I even bother telling him the truth? I shook my head. "I think you're really nice…"

"But, I'm too…insert cliché here…" he drawled.

Was I really doing to him what everyone had done to me? "No, I mean… I'm messing this up," I said rubbing my forehead.

"Yes, you are," he leaned forward. "Look, Autumn I suppose you've been really disappointed and it's easier to let it go than take a risk."

I nodded. "I'm not that good at this. Trusting, hoping, taking risks."

"Isn't autumn itself a risk?"

"I don't understand."

"The trees let go in hope that something new will bloom."

I didn't say anything. I felt something in me begin to awaken. Hope. But, I wanted to be sure. I had to be sure.

I leaned forward. "One month. Take a month. Pray about it and if you still want me to take the risk-"

"I'm ready to take the risk," he said without hesitation.

I laughed. "Ok, maybe I should rephrase it. If you still want me to take the risk after a month, then you can send me a letter."

"A letter?" he said raising a brow.

"Yeah, you're a soldier, don't you write letters?"

"Yeah, I just thought you'd want a call."

"That's too easy."

He looked at me for a while and then laughed. "I'm looking forward to sending that letter."

I was too. But the letter never came.

11

Isaac and Isaiah. Laughter and God's generosity. If Rachel and Keith cried any more tears of gratitude, then both of their eyes would've swollen shut. Holding both boys felt like a dream, but at the same time almost like déjà vu. I had imagined this moment so many times with her that I felt like I had already been here.

Keith had taken some time off of work to help Rachel, because it was double the diapers, crying, feedings, and laundry. Who says that God's blessings don't come with work? Ellie and I planned on going over some days to help out when Keith went back to work.

It's funny how when babies come into the picture how time seems to speed up. Every month hurries along and you realize they've made another milestone. And before I knew it, the boys were nine months and it had been two years since the planting.

And still nothing came up from the ground.

Ellie's vines had twined together in the formation of a tree although none of us still couldn't tell what that tree was. Even Camila's new seed had sprung up, revealing itself to be a mango tree. Abuela had quickly figured that one out.

There were things I didn't care about knowing anymore: why those seeds didn't grow and what seeds they were.

Call it a hope deferred, but I found my days becoming laborious. I felt stifled at work, at church, I felt like I was gasping for air, trying to figure out where my source of oxygen would come from. When I was asked whether I would be returning for the next school year, I did something I never thought I would or could do. I said no. Everyone thought I was crazy, how could I leave my job with nothing lined up after? Worse, when I told them I would be taking the next three months of summer, nope not to find another job, but to go home. I was going back to Michigan, not to the city, but the country. Even Rachel thought I was nuts to go back to Michigan to the cold.

Forget about what everyone thought of me, I thought I was going a bit crazy. It really didn't make any sense and the only person I could think to talk to was Sister Blossom cause from day one she's been making me do things that don't make sense.

I pulled up to her little place in South Miami. I came and picked her up every week for church and every week I noticed all the life outside of it, and that didn't compare to the life in the backyard. It was this ordered garden. But today, it looked a bit chaotic to me. There were bushes growing up everywhere. Greens, pinks, purples, whites, yellows and reds, all seemed tangled together.

I knocked on the door and I heard her voice asking who it was. I knew she'd be shocked to hear from me unannounced on a Thursday afternoon.

She opened the door. "Autumn," she said with a smile.

"Hi," I said swallowing nervously. "I just needed someone to talk to."

She opened her door wide, beckoning me to come inside. I stepped in and went to her living room and sat in the chair she usually had for me.

"You want anything to eat or drink?"

"No, thank you."

She came and sat down, holding on to the arms of the chair. "What's going on?"

I told her about resigning and about leaving for Michigan. I didn't really know why I was here. I'm sure she would tell me the same things everyone else told me. She might even tell me I needed to stay to take care of my non-existent plant. She listened as usual and I was prepared for her to shoot off her usual barrage of soul seeking questions.

"I think you should go."

I must not have heard her right. "I'm sorry, what?"

"You wanted my advice. I think you should go."

"That's it? No other words?"

"Nope," she said, getting up out of her chair. "I've got some gloves and shears. Do you mind helping me prune my garden?"

"No," I said absentmindedly, still processing the strangeness of this moment.

But, I didn't say anything to her. Not even when I was outside mimicking her movements as she pruned her garden. "You see that tree over there?" she said, pointing to a small cherry tree.

"Yeah, what about it?"

"I remember when I first planted that tree. But it wouldn't grow. It was like it was stunted somehow. And then in one of the hurricanes, it got knocked down. And instead of tossing it, I replanted it in a different place and it grew more than it ever did in the first soil it was in."

I looked over at the plant, it's green leaves and cherries in red dots, some of them still developing and so they were an orangey-red color. "So, you don't think I'm crazy for just picking up and going? I don't even know when I'll be back for sure."

She continued pruning her plants. "Oh no, sometimes we have to move out of our familiar places if we ever plan to come back to them. Sometimes we don't come back to them. Only God knows. Would Abram have become the father of many nations if he'd stayed where he was?"

"But, I'm not like him. I love Miami. I want to come back, I just need some time to just figure stuff out."

She nodded. "Come here," she said, holding out the shears for me. "Cut this off," she said, pointing to a branch of flowers on her bougainvillea.

"What? Are you sure? This branch is filled with flowers."

"Cut it," she said.

I did exactly what she said although I almost winced while doing it. Why cut off a perfectly good stem?

She smiled. "It will grow back, better and stronger. That branch was crowding out the rest of the flowers. This time it won't."

"I'm trying to understand this whole process. I know everyone's plant means something. I'm trying to understand what mine means."

"Ask and it will be given to you, seek and you will find; knock and the door will be opened."

I chuckled. "Yes, I know."

Her chuckles mingled with mine. "I know that you think you know. When have you truly prayed without wavering, without doubting? Have you ever thanked God in advance for what you prayed for, imagined it, told people about it?"

I didn't respond, and she continued. "Then you don't know."

I opened my mouth to say something in defense. But I

had nothing.

"Don't worry, if you'd like, I can take care of your seed for you until you come back."

"I told you I didn't know if I was coming back for good."

She smiled slyly. "You'll be back Autumn. You're not the type to leave your work undone."

"Are you sure you're not running away?" Rachel said to me a week later as I threw Isaac in the air and heard his squeals and giggles. I kissed his chubby cheek, even though some baby slobber was on his cheek.

"No, I'm not running away Rae. I just need some time to figure things out, that's all."

She bounced Isaiah on her leg. "I'm just gonna miss you. Plus, what if Matt comes back?"

I laughed. "What if he does? I'm not waiting around for Matt or for anyone. If he wanted to get in contact with me he would've."

"I told you I could've talked to him. It's so weird though Autumn, cause he told Keith he had a great time. He was so excited. He was talking like you were the girl of his dreams or something."

"Dreams....Nightmares...they both happen when you're asleep."

Her eyes narrowed. "You two are either stubborn or just plain dumb. You have each other's phone numbers, and if for some reason he lost your number, there's Facebook or Instagram and you guys can talk to each other there, instead of silently stalking each other's posts."

I held Isaac on my hip. "And I told you I didn't want anyone to meddle. He seems quite happy without me. That's it. Leave things where they are."

I had once gone on his social media and seen picture of him happy in Italy with his Air Force friends chilling. "He's fine without me. I promise. He probably went home after that date and said, dang that girl was nuts," I said, smiling at Rachel.

She wasn't smiling. "I hate when you do that," she said. "You make fun, but I know you. It hurts."

"I'm fine, Rachel. I promise. It was one date."

She nodded and spoke to Isaiah in a baby voice. "Tell Auntie Autumn not to go to cold Michigan. Miami is the best."

I smiled. "Isaiah, can't say all of that, so I guess my plan still stays intact." I sat down across from her and put Isaac in my lap. He didn't stay for long and wiggled to crawl on the floor. Before long, his brother followed suit.

"You can come anytime you want. Bring the boys. It's quiet there. Lots of nature. I'm sure after a couple weeks I'll be itching to see you all."

She swallowed. "Tell me the truth, why did you resign, why are you leaving?"

I sighed. "We always dreamed of coming here to Miami together, and we did it Rae. I came here thinking it would be everything I dreamed of my whole life living in Detroit, and it was, for a while. Rae, I got everything I asked for, everything except one thing, and I let it keep me from God. Now, I think maybe I never really knew what I wanted, or rather, what I needed." I took a breath. "Sometimes you just gotta go home and start over."

She sighed in surrender. "Have you prayed about it?"

I nodded. "Yes."

"Then go. God is here, and God is there. But sometimes, he'll move at a specific place, at a specific time, for a specific reason. If he's leading you home, who am I to stop you?"

12

I grew up on the east side of Detroit. But every summer we'd drive out to the border of Michigan and Indiana where my grandfather owned acres of rolling land. The apple orchard spread out across the land and the lake on the other side was surrounded by young black gum trees.

I used to love visiting there when we were younger, and my dad would always talk about retiring there. I didn't have any siblings, but my parents didn't need to have anyone else for me considering that Rachel was always over the house. I used to hate coming to the orchard in the summer cause that meant I was away from

Rachel, but when we turned thirteen her parents started letting her come with us. It was such a difference than the noisy city life, here Rachel and I could get out on a canoe and paddle and swim. As soon as it was nearing time to go back to school, we all headed back to Detroit.

When my grandfather passed away, my dad took ownership of the property. But, he was still working and had to have farm hands take care of it while he was away. Unfortunately, they weren't being as diligent as they could, because our apples were going bad, and my dad could see that the orchard was in disarray. That orchard had been passed down for generations; from former slaves who had finally had the opportunity to own a piece of land they could call theirs and make it into a business.

My Dad resigned from his job and moved down there with my mom permanently about five years after I had moved to Miami. I thought that they would hate it for sure. That soon they would be back in Detroit, but they loved it, the slow pace, the quiet, and the stillness.

There wasn't even cell service out here. Thank God they had gotten Wi-Fi so that I could still communicate with them. I drove along the road, passing corn and wheat fields, before I made the turn into our property. I parked at the front, and as I exited the car, my mom ran out of the house and pulled me into a tight embrace and I let out a breath I didn't realize I had been holding.

The first month I was there, I'll be honest, I don't think much changed. It was like I was thawing out. Every night I would sit outside looking out at the trees because everything around me was pitch black, yet the hundreds of light bugs crowded the trees by the lake looked like twinkling stars and I found myself praying for Sister Blossom, Ellie, Rachel, Valentina, Camila, and Matt.

At first, I told myself I was only praying for him because it felt better than being angry with him. But, I liked it. It gave me peace. I didn't pray for his letters, or calls, not even for a DM, for all I knew he was probably with someone else by now. It'd been a year. Sometimes I worried if he was still alive, but I was sure Rachel would tell me if Keith found out anything like that. I just prayed for him, for his well-being, and something about that felt nice, something let me know that God heard me, even in the darkness each night that I prayed.

One night, it must've been a week after I'd come home, my dad joined me out there.

"Hey Leaf, what's up?" My Dad had been calling me

leaf since I could remember. First, it was that I was his autumn leaf and then it just shortened to "Leaf". My dad now was completely grey at just his mid-fifties. He was still strong enough to handle all of the tasks out on the orchard though. Everyone said I looked like my mother with my petite frame and curly hair. But, everyone always knew I had gotten my father's brown eyes.

"Nothing much."

"You've been spending a lot of time out here by yourself at night. You sure some guy in Miami didn't break your heart and that's not why you're here, sitting in the dark, counting stars?"

I smiled. "You gonna take out your shotgun and scare him?"

"You want me to?"

I grinned. "Nah, it wasn't a guy. It wasn't anyone really. I just needed to come home for a while."

"Your house is fine though?"

"Yeah, Ellie and Rachel are taking turns watching it for me. Keeping it from getting dusty and gross."

There were so many stars out here. I almost forgot how many stars there were living in the city.

"You're so sad. That's not my girl."

I rested my head on his shoulder remembering something he used to say to me as a kid. "I know Daddy. I think I just needed to come home and remember that there's so many stars."

He caught on and continued. "No, you only need to remember that God knows each of their names."

I finished. "And that he likes mine even more."

Ellie was the first to come visit me. She came in August since I told her that she should come before the snow starts.

We walked through the orchard with our baskets as I told her which ones were ok to pick and which ones needed to be left on the tree a little longer. Right now, it was harvest time for the Red Delicious apples for eating and next month would be the Red Rome apples for cooking and then in October the Green Granny Smith apples. "This is so weird to see you like this," she said.

"Like what?"

"In an orchard. In this country setting. I'm used to us being in the city," she said. "But, I love it. I can see why you're here."

"It's definitely different," I said with an airy laugh.

"You're different."

I laughed. "Really?" I said sarcastically. "Ellie, it's only been two months."

"I'm telling you Autumn, you may not notice it, but you're different," she said as we continued walking.

"I hope it's in a good way."

"Of course, you look….more peaceful."

I nodded. "I feel more peaceful." The smell of apples was strong and sweet as we walked through the orchard, stepping over the apples that had fallen to the ground and started rotting. They would fall and continue to fertilize the earth. Nothing was ever wasted, it was like the Earth understood that all things work together, even though humans didn't.

"So, is this what we all need to do? Run away to the quiet?"

I chuckled. "No. I mean the setting has helped, but it's not just that…it's… it's that I'm being quiet and now I can finally hear."

She smiled. "I brought you something she said reaching for the book bag on her back and pulling out a journal. "I brought you a new prayer journal. I remember you started to use the one Sister Blossom gave you, but then you just fell off. I figured you might want to start using it again."

I took it and looked at the cover with a bamboo print. How do I explain to her that my prayers for years were less like prayers and more like complaints and demands? "Thank you it's really cute," I said. "I'm not sure if before I came here if I've really prayed in a long time."

"Well, thank God you have others praying for you."

"Yeah, thank God."

I looked at the variations of red on the apple in my hand. It had shades of cherry, rose and garnet all embedded in it.

"I figured out what my plant is," Ellie said. "Right before I came here I noticed some light purple blooms coming from it. I did a Google search. It's called wisteria." She took out her phone showing me the delicate drooping lavender blooms.

"Wisteria?" I asked. I'd never heard of it.

"Yeah, it says it's a plant that means welcome. I was a little confused. I mean, why did she give me a wisteria tree?"

"Sister Blossom isn't the easiest person to

understand."

I wanted to ask her if she'd seen anything different with my plant. Had it come out of the ground yet?

"Sister Blossom and I have been alternating watering yours. Nothing yet, but something will come."

I wasn't sure if I meant it, but I wanted to mean it, so I said, "Yeah, something will come."

She inhaled deeply. "I have something to tell you. I didn't tell you before because I just wasn't sure how to. Everything has happened so fast-"

I knew. I knew what she was going to say. "You met someone," I interrupted.

"Yeah. I did. His name is Jesse. I met him in Nashville a couple weeks ago. He's really nice, I like him."

I wasn't bothered that she'd met someone. Other than her sister coming home, there was nothing more I wanted for Ellie than for her to meet someone who'd treat her with the respect she deserved. What bothered me was that everyone felt like they couldn't tell me these things, like they had to hope I didn't have a meltdown. I couldn't blame them. How many times had Ellie heard me complain in a jealous fit how everyone was meeting Mr. Right but me?

I opened my arms and gave her a big hug. "I'm so happy for you. I want you to believe that," I said, releasing her and smiling warmly.

She looked like a weight came off of her shoulders. I smirked. "Now tell me all about him cause I need to know how much I have to threaten him to treat you well."

We continued our walk as she told me that he was an automotive engineer just in Nashville for the weekend. He lived in Long Beach, California, but was in Nashville for the weekend when he and Ellie met in the airport. She been sitting there reading through this book Sister Blossom had given her when he'd struck up a conversation with her about it. Since then, they'd been on three dates, dozens of phone calls and thousands of text messages. Her excitement was contagious, and I made a mental note to add them to my prayer list, and Jesse to my hit list should Ellie call me with a broken heart or broken commitments to God.

Ellie's stay with me wasn't too long. Only four days and then she was going back home to Miami for a week before she had to head off to London. I waited for her message back when she got home. She did get home safely and underneath the wisteria tree sat Emmy reading a book, detoxed, her smile as brilliant as ever based on the picture Ellie sent me. It turns out the wisteria tree wasn't for Ellie at all. That welcome was always meant for Emmy.

13

Lord, forgive me for all the times I've doubted you and been angry or frustrated with you. All of it stems from a lack of trust. I know I don't deserve it, but I really need your help. I don't want to call it a thorn, but I'm having a hard time dealing with singleness. I do try daily to make the best of it. Well, some days I try my best. My heart yearns for companionship, for children, to share my life with someone who loves me and who I can love back. And it really hurts that each time I get hopeful that my prayers are being answered, that rejection hits me in the face and I'm back at square one questioning what's wrong with me?

I don't want to feel this way anymore. I know you care. I know you see. I know you see how much I've tried to please you in this area. I know you hear each prayer. I know despite my pain that you're good and that you're here. Even as I'm sobbing, you're here.

Please just send comfort. I would love for this season of singleness to be over, but I don't know if that's your plan. Give me a content spirit, that no matter what you decide to do, that my eyes will be on you and my mind will be in perfect peace.

You know what's best for me, even though sometimes I wish I knew your plans in full detail. Help me to hold on to your hand and take one step at a time with you. Help me to trust your plan, even when I don't understand it and to remember that you love me.

In Jesus Name,

Amen

And just like that the words and the melody came to me as I sat by the piano.

You planted a seed
That I knew was me
But how could it be
That you would choose me

You tilled the soil of my life so patiently
Grace to grace you held my hand faithfully
Transformed my worries into peace

Springing from the ground you helped me see
I am blooming.

I hadn't written a song in 5 years and suddenly in 30 minutes I had a musical arrangement and words down. And somehow it made sense to me: something I had tried to do for years, God had done in minutes.

You don't really see autumn in Miami. No not Autumn as in me. Autumn as in fall, the season. I guess, you could say that all these years you couldn't see Autumn (me) in Miami either. But, as October came with its crisp air and fiery leaves, I realized I could see Autumn quite clearly. I looked back at my reflection, my brown hair had darkened a bit now that I wasn't in the Miami sun as much. My face was clear, except for the few faded acne scars on my cheeks that resembled freckles. My skin had always been on the darker side, the color of chestnuts, somehow, I could tell that my skin had a glow to it that it didn't have before. My eyes no longer had those dark circles under them that I always chalked up to a busy schedule. I hadn't gone on a skin care regimen, it wasn't like I was eating a lot healthier than before.

A weight was now gone. I wasn't really worried about anything. Not singlehood, not paying bills, not my health, not about my career, or…anything. That's the thing about worry. People always think they can just contain it and worry about one thing. But it's like a disease, it spreads to other areas and before you know it, you're worried about everything and you can't sleep because of it.

Worrying about what would happen next kept me from enjoying anything that could ever be happening now. I couldn't be happy for others the way I truly wanted to be, because my own worries turned into jealousy and the moment something good happened for me, I worried about when it would go bad.

There was a knock at the door and my mom stuck her head in. my mother and I always fooled people with our ages. She still looked young with her curly hair pulled back into a bun. Only the slight wrinkles near her eyes gave her away.

"When are we leaving to go get Rachel from the airport?"

"I'll be ready in just a few," I said, combing through my hair.

She stepped inside the room and closed the door behind her. She held out her hand for the comb I had and started to comb through my hair. "When you were little you used to love when I combed through your hair."

I laughed. "You just knew how to do it right. Not too rough and you always got out all the tangles."

She continued combing, detangling. "It's funny when you have a child and they're small, it's like you know exactly how to fix all their problems, but as they get older, the problems get more complex and you don't really know how to fix them anymore. All you can do is pray."

I didn't say anything. I was thinking about what she was saying and giving her time to continue.

"You know I'm glad to see you. I always am. But, tell me the truth, why did you really come here?"

"I just... I needed time. To get quiet for a while." I cleared my throat. "Mom, I lost who I was. I wanted so many things and they weren't bad things. They were good things. But, what I needed, I didn't want as much."

She nodded. "Nothing and no one can replace God."

"Yes, I know that now."

A joy swelled up in me to see Rachel, Keith, Isaac

and Isaiah. It'd only been four months since I'd last seen them and already they were walking and looked so much bigger than I'd remembered them. The boys still had their creamy complexions with these afros full of curls.

Rachel and I videochatted with each other all the time and I saw the boys, but somehow seeing them in person made me realize how much of an illusion it was to see them on a screen. They were more hesitant to come to me than they were before when they'd seen me all the time, but eventually the both of them didn't mind coming into my arms and accepting my kisses and tickles. Of course, in a couple of minutes they were ready to go back to their parents.

I was happy that Keith was with Rachel for this trip. Rachel never complained much about Keith's work schedule, but I knew she didn't like him gone so often and she was always happier when he was around. I always joked that he replaced me as the coffee to her crème. They came right in time for the granny smith apple picking season, so Rachel and I walked down the orchard with me holding Isaiah and Rachel holding Isaac. They were identical twins, except Isaiah had a small birthmark on his hand.

"How has everything at home been?" I asked, as we strolled through the orchard, me still holding Isaiah as she held Isaac.

"It's been good. A bit lonely with you gone, but Eliie comes by and I'll pick up Sister Blossom to come over and just keep me company. The boys love her."

"Of course they do," I said laughing. "Sometimes I think if it wasn't for her, would they be here? She was the one that got you praying and believing and planting baby's breath."

She grinned. "Yes. I actually had a shoot done with the boys running around outside in the baby's breath. Once I get the photos back I'll mail you a framed picture of them."

"Please!" I pleaded. "I'm definitely putting it up in the house."

"Your house here or in Miami?" Rachel asked cheekily.

I rolled my eyes. "I don't have an answer to that."

She changed the subject. "Have you talked to her since you've been here?"

"Talked to who?"

"Sister Blossom."

I bounced Isaiah up and down. "To be honest, I'm not sure what to say to her. It feels weird you know."

"Why?"

"I'm not sure why. Maybe it's all in my head, but I feel like she might tell me that she told me so."

She laughed. "Oh, my goodness! I felt like I just had déjà vu! You definitely said the same thing in college."

"I did not!" I said laughing back.

"You did too, remember when you dated that guy that all of us told you not to. When he ditched you and left you in Paris, you didn't tell me for a whole week after you came home. I'm still mad about that too, cause I could've taken his ticket. He had you out there wasting money. But, you didn't tell me, you said, 'I just felt like you were gonna say I told you so'".

I shook my head. Rachel was right. He did waste my money, not just break my heart. Also, I did tell her that I didn't tell her cause she would've lectured me. I remember. Even though no one knew about our plan to elope. Everyone knew about our relationship and when it was over, I didn't know how to tell everyone that they'd been right about him. My pride.

"It's my pride, isn't it?"

"You said it, I didn't."

I rolled my eyes again. "Ok, ok, I got it. I'll call her." Isaiah was wriggling in my arms trying to pick an apple. I leaned over and let him tug at one. Isaac saw his brother and tried to do the same. Finally, Isaiah was able to wrestle it from the tree and I pulled the apple away from him before he could just take a huge bite into it. I would have to bring the apples inside and have them cleaned and cut for the boys.

Before I knew it, I had two stubborn boys crying because they wanted to take a full bite of an apple with their tender teeth. They didn't know if these apples had worms or were clean and they didn't care because they didn't understand. Even though they cried and wailed, I couldn't give it to them until the apples were ready for them. So that walk back to the house, the process of cleaning and inspecting the apples only took about fifteen minutes, but it seemed like an hour with their hollering. And when those sliced apples were given to them, they stopped crying and they smiled and chewed as if they couldn't remember anything from before.

The boys and the apples were kind of like me and God. I wanted something, and it wasn't that God didn't want to give it to me, he just had to make sure it was right before he did.

I leaned over and kissed both of their foreheads. "You guys are some big babies and I'm the biggest."

It was the night before Rachel's family would head home. I left out at my normal time to sit outside at night and watch the stars and write in my prayer journal. Fall would be over soon, and it would be too cold to do this at night. As I drew on a fall coat and walked down the hall, I heard Rachel's voice.

"Wait, don't leave me," she said, pulling on a coat and scarf and following me.

We both headed outside and sat on the bench that my grandfather had built long ago that over looked the lake.

"I remember how much fun we used to have at this place every summer," she said.

I smiled. "Yes, catching the light bugs," she said as we looked at the light bugs in the trees resembling Christmas decorations.

It was dark out here, but I could see the glow of her

light skin and hair. She gasped in awe. "I can see why you escaped here."

"Miami wasn't prison."

"No, but somehow I think it might've been for you."

I shook my head. "No, I was in a prison in my mind. No matter where I went it would've been the same."

"Gosh, Ellie was right. You're different. I love this version of you." She looped her arm in mine. "So, when are you coming home?"

I really didn't know. I couldn't give anyone a time frame. I felt like when I was ready I would know. "I'm not sure. Just know that any day I could pop back up."

She sighed. "Well, that's a downer, but I do like surprises."

I smiled. "I'm starting to like them too."

"Guess what?" she asked.

"What?"

"I decided to start work again," Rachel had gone to school for advertising and somehow had gotten into stationary design after her own wedding. She had a pretty good earning making wedding stationary until she toned things down having to take care of the boys.

"That's great! You know you're my favorite

designer."

"I'm glad you think so," she said. "Cause I've already designed your whole suite. It's got a bit of a rustic flair."

"What?" I asked laughing. "Why would you make it rustic?"

"I'm at home, I'm bored, you ditched me to pick apples, go canoeing and stargazing," she said grinning. "Listen, just because it didn't work out with the others doesn't mean it won't ever. God has a purpose, even for our pain, if we give it to him."

Rachel was one of the strongest people I'd known. Growing up you would've thought she would've broken under the abuse she'd suffered, but instead she'd used that to help others. She was constantly sharing her testimony. She worked closely with charities that worked with girls recovering from sexual abuse. She partnered with charities rescuing victims of sexual trafficking. She helped God give her a purpose after her pain.

"Whose name did you put as the groom?" I asked.

"You know who," she said.

I rolled my eyes and groaned.

"I'm still holding out hope. There has to be a reason. You just won't let me ask him and I would be sneaky, but

I'm trying to respect your wishes."

"Thank you for respecting my wishes."

"You sure you don't want me to-

"Thank you, Rachel, for respecting my wishes," I said putting my foot down.

She sighed. "Ok, ok, I got it. You guys were perfect though. I really thought I was right about him. Keith and I were so sure. You know we'd never set you up to get hurt. Keith actually told me when he tried to bring you up that Matt didn't really want to talk about it. Matt said the date obviously didn't go as well as he thought it did."

What was that supposed to mean? He was the one that never talked to me again. I sighed. "Everything happens for a reason, Rae." I looked up at the stars. "I have a secret though, I pray for him sometimes. Not really for us to be together. It seems dumb to pray for that. It was one day, one date. Why should he matter so much? But, I do like praying for him. It feels peaceful to pray for him."

She reached in her pocket. "I brought something for you," she said, pulling out a small booklet. "I designed this booklet for you. It's some really important stories of faith and scriptures of faith. I thought it might help you on the good days and especially on the rough days."

I turned it over in my hand. I couldn't see the design in the dark. "Thank you so much. I know I'll need it. Winter is coming."

The next morning, we woke up early to take the Anderson's to the airport. The two and a half hour drive was light hearted and fun as the boys slept most of it or watched their nursery rhymes. Keith, Rachel and I reminisced about college, they filled me in on everything happening at Harvest. I liked the church here, but I did miss my church back in Miami a lot. They told me that the praise team was doing really well, and I was happy, I had been really concerned about that. I still watched the sermons from Miami every week online, so I still felt connected in a way.

"Yo, Autumn I need you back in Miami. Rachel still doesn't get all my Jamie Foxx show references," Keith said.

I laughed. "Sorry man, she grew up watching Martin with me, you'll have to stick to that."

When we arrived at the airport and their entire

luggage was unloaded, before Rachel walked into the airport, she gave me a tight squeeze and said, "Maybe he's only been delayed because your faith has been weak. Keep praying for him. Don't give up. From the moment I saw you two, I knew. I just knew." She didn't really give me an opportunity to respond. She just walked away, carrying her suitcases with her.

I wanted to ask what did she know? But I knew the answer to that. What I didn't know was how did she know? And how did she believe it so strongly?

14

"Now faith is the substance of things hoped for, the evidence of things not seen. For by it the elders obtained a good report. Through faith we understand that the worlds were framed by the word of God, so that things which are seen were not made of things which do appear," I read aloud and paused as I stared out my window at the hills covered in inches of pearlescent snow.

If I believed that God created the stars that I see each night, how could I not believe that he could do anything else?

I dialed Sister Blossom's number after six months of being in Michigan.

"Hello?" she said.

"Hi, Sister Blossom, it's Autumn."

"Hi, Autumn," she said excitedly. "I've been waiting

to hear your voice!"

Why was she so excited? I'd avoided her for six months. She should be mad at me. I deserved it. "I know I should've called a long time ago and I want to apologize for that."

"Oh, yes, well, I'm glad to hear from you now, so tell me, how's Michigan?"

"It's been really good. I've been feeling more like myself than I ever have."

"Music to my ears!"

I chuckled. "I've been writing songs too."

"Well, I need to hear them, you can just send those to Rachel or Ellie and they'll get them to me.

"I promise I will." There was an awkward silence and I realized how little I usually talked with her. She was always the one initiating conversation and asking questions. "How's my plant doing?"

"It's coming along you know, it's doing quite well, I'd say."

"What's it look like?"

"I don't know yet, it's still hiding itself underground, but it's gonna be a sight to see," she chuckled to herself. "A sight to see."

I wasn't annoyed by her saying that, I chuckled at her words. "I don't think anyone is more eager to see exactly what this thing will be."

"You'll see my dear, I can guarantee it."

"How can you believe so strongly all the time Sister Blossom? I mean, how did you get to the place where you have so much faith about everything? You were right about Rachel and Camila and Valentina. My God, you were right about Emmy coming home. How?"

"I'm not doing anything God hasn't empowered me to do or you to do. You shall have whatever you say. Anything you ask according to God's will is done. Whether you see it immediately or later, it's done. You can speak to the mountain or the fig tree or the sea."

"How do you know what's his will?"

"If it's in his word, it's in his will."

"No, I get that. I mean, how do you know exactly what God wants for you, like what college to go to, what major to pick, how many kids you'll have, or if you'll have them at all, or if your sister will come back here, or you'll see her in heaven, or for me, who I'll marry, or whether I'll ever be married?"

"I see," she sighed. "God is not as mysterious as we

think he is. Yes, there are things he withholds from us. To build our faith. If we knew everything we wouldn't need him. But, he loves to reveal himself to us. Yes, sometimes he does it over time, but the closer you draw to God, is the more you hear him, you recognize his voice. You'll begin to understand that the desire he's placed in you lines up with his word, so now you pray for him to reveal specifically what he would like you to do about that, who you should consider and not consider."

"I want to get it right this time. I don't want to be wrong Sister Blossom, and I'm afraid that if I start saying stuff in faith that I'll be wrong. I'll look stupid and I'll make people doubt God, because I said he was going to do something and he didn't, because I was wrong."

"There's grace for that Autumn," she sighed. "You are so weighed down by cares that you shouldn't be. Be like a child again. Believe that your father can do any and everything again. How did you feel when Rachel's boys were born, or when Emmy came home, or when Camila chose Columbia over Georgetown, or when Valentina went to design school?"

"I was so happy. I don't know how to explain it. I wasn't jealous. I felt like I was celebrating with them. If it could happen for them then God could do it for me."

"Yes! You got it!" she quieted down again. "Your breakthrough is never just for you. So believe enough to say it to yourself and then say it to another person."

I didn't cry in this conversation with her like I did with all the others. But, I hung up the phone so scared, because I knew this was going to be hard.

By faith Noah, being warned of God by things not seen as yet, moved with fear, prepared an ark to the saving of his house; by which he condemned the world, and became heir of the righteousness which is by faith.

This morning at church they were speaking about Noah. I've heard the story all my life and it hit me like a ton of bricks now. He got a word from God, he was convinced it was God, and he did exactly as God told him to. The precise measurements God told him to make the ark, all the animals God told him to get in the ark, he did it all. Even when he didn't even understand what rain was. It took anywhere from 55 to 75 for years from the time God told Noah to the first raindrop to fall and he spent all this time building and looking even more crazy by telling everyone what would happen....and I was having trouble believing I could tell someone that I wouldn't be single forever.

Does God always show us how foolish we can be?

By April, the land began to thaw out. And by May, I could truly see that spring was in full bloom, there were light pinks and yellows everywhere I went. I had read through the entire booklet that Rachel had given me. I saw myself in Sarah's laughter and in Abraham and Sarah's agreement to try things their way. I saw myself in Gideon's continued pleas for God to prove himself in a different way. In Moses, who said, "I don't speak so well". I saw myself in the spies that said that the giants were too big. But, now I see myself in Elijah who said go back again to check for the rain, in the Israelites who walked around the wall and shouted, and in Mary who said, "be it unto me according to thy will."

And I knew I was ready to go home now.

15

The I-74 drive home was different than it was when I was going to Michigan last June. It was one year later and now three years since the planting. Even though, I knew it had been a long time since I had put that seed into the ground, it also seemed like it had been just a few days. Kind of like Jacob's love for Rachel. Now it was my love for God and even more stronger, his love for me.

I wanted to surprise Ellie first, so as I pulled into her neighborhood I called her.

"Hey what's up?"

"Hey," I said, coming out of my car and walking up to her front door. "I sent something to your house and it said it delivered. Can you check outside and see if it got there?"

"Yeah sure," she said. I waited in excited anticipation as the sound of the lock turned and she opened. Her surprised screams filled the air before she started crying. "You're home," she sobbed as she hugged me tightly, her braids falling onto my shoulders. "I can't believe you're actually home."

Rachel was the one that had quite the surprise for me when she opened the door with a dress that displayed a protruding stomach.

I put my hand over my mouth, "How many months? I thought they said you couldn't have anymore?"

"Six months. They were wrong," she said, answering my questions. "They didn't have the last word."

"How could you not tell me?"

She shook her head. "I honestly wanted to wait until I hit my second trimester. Then I hit that, and I just said "Hey, if this girl doesn't come home then I'll guilt her into coming home."

I laughed. "Girl or Boy?"

"Girl!" she squealed excitedly. "The baby shower is gonna be next month. I was actually calling you this month to tell you, I was getting tired of hiding my stomach in the video chat."

She chattered about her plans for the shower before she threw this part in, "Keith called Matt to invite him. He says he's coming. Are you still going to want to come?"

Did I? Just the thought of him being there made me nervous. Could you imagine how nervous I would be the day of?

"Rachel, I wouldn't miss your baby shower for anything. Just don't sign me up for any more games," I said jokingly.

"You know, I don't know, the hostess just might ask you to," she said.

I rolled my eyes. It seemed like I was always rolling my eyes around Rachel.

"Listen, you haven't let me meddle not once in all this time!"

"I'm very grateful you haven't."

She sat back. "You know what? So am I…. now when it happens none of us will be able to take credit for it."

"Exactly."

Rachel always knew I would come home. I don't

think she ever doubted that for a second. She had never given me my framed picture of the boys in the garden amongst the baby's breath. But she had it there waiting for me. She told me she was going to mail it to me. But, she decided wouldn't give it to me until I was home, so I could hang it in my home.

Next, I made my way to Camila and Valentina's house. I knew they'd be home for the summer. They screamed in excitement when they opened the door, and Abuela rushed to whip something up for me to eat. I looked outside at their backyard and saw that Camila's mango tree was filled and that the bougainvillea were still bright and beautiful.

Abuela chattered to me in Spanish telling me to take as many mangoes as I wanted. That much I understood.

"Gracias, Abuela," I said.

"De nada," she said back.

"We have a surprise for you," Camila said. Valentina elbowed her gently. "Well, Valentina has a surprise for you, but I helped. A little."

"Close your eyes," Valentina said.

I did as they asked. "Is it pastelitos?" I called out.

"No!" came their twin replies.

"Um…. Is it croquettas? You know I like croquettas."

"It's better than that," Valentina said.

"What could be better?" I asked jokingly.

"Ok, open your eyes," Camila said, and when I did I saw a V-neck silk wedding dress with a floral lace across the bust.

I didn't have words. I stared ahead with my mouth agape. I just started to cry. I didn't plan to. I felt so flushed, happy and loved.

"Your mom actually picked the sketch out. I emailed her the designs and she picked this one for you."

That just made me sob even more.

"I don't even have a boyfriend," I said laughing and crying. I held the dress in awe of how perfect it was.

"Well, it's about time you got one with a dress like that hanging in your closet," Camila said.

"Sí, mucha felicidad y bebés para ti," Abuela said, kissing my cheek and wishing me happiness and lots of babies.

"Solo tres," I responded back to her.

Who would've thought I would've come home to so much in just one day?

16

Sister Blossom was my last stop. I pulled up to her house. Her garden was back in immaculate condition and I rang the doorbell.

She smiled warmly, and I realized how much I had missed her. In fact, I think I felt more joy in seeing her now than I felt with any of my friends. Even more joy than the wedding dress. "You finally decided to come home."

I nodded and stepped inside at her invitation. "Yes. It was time to come home."

She looked at me closely. "Oh Autumn, I see it now, you've bloomed so beautifully."

I smiled, and she continued. "To everything there is a season, and a time to every purpose under heaven. Now you bloom and one day the leaves will fall again. Don't forget what you've learned now." I nodded, but I didn't really understand then when she'd said it.

All we did was talk about everything I had learned and seen and experienced in Michigan. I showed her the dress Valentina had made for me, I even tried it on and twirled for her and she just looked so happy to see me happy.

That evening I had gone home exhausted and ready to go to bed. It was dark to go out in the backyard, but I went anyway with a pitcher of water and turned on the lights. There was nothing coming out of the ground and I sighed and poured some water in the ground where I remembered burying my seed. The ground now looked normal after three years, it was covered with grass.

"If I'm blooming, then it's about time you bloom too," I said quietly.

I went upstairs and got ready for bed. Rachel, Ellie and Sister Blossom had done an amazing job of keeping this place clean and tidy. It didn't look abandoned and dusty. It looked just like I'd left it. I was truly in their debt and had to get them something nice to say thank you for all they'd done.

I was so exhausted that it wasn't long before I drifted off to sleep. I woke up the next morning, the sun shining brightly in my face. I went downstairs to make breakfast.

I started to make a cup of tea, putting a tea bag into a mug. As I went grab some sugar from the cupboard, I spied something sticking up out of the ground in my backyard. It couldn't be. I stepped closer to the window. Yes, there was definitely something coming out of the ground. I raced outside and bent down to look at it more closely. It was a stick. A green stick, with a slim leaf coming out of it. No, it wasn't just a stick….it was bamboo.

I laughed. Sister Blossom had given me bamboo seeds. I grabbed my phone and started taking pictures of it before searching it online. Bamboo stays beneath the soil for 3-5 years and then spontaneously emerges from the ground, growing at a rapid pace. I laughed even more and went to text the girls when my doorbell rang. I went to the door and my mailman Dennis greeted me.

"Autumn, I haven't seen you in a long time. I was worried that you'd moved."

"Hey Dennis, yeah I was spending a year with my parents in another state. I had some friends picking up mail for me."

He nodded. "Oh, I mean I saw that the mail I put in there for the most part was gone after a few days. But, I didn't feel comfortable giving these letters to just anyone. I don't know, they seemed important. All the way from overseas."

He put the stack of letters in my hand. "Well, these letters have been delivered to you dating back two years. Seems they've been going to the wrong address. The person waited a while to send them to the post office. We caught up with the problem not too long ago, but I kept coming by, and didn't see you. I told myself this was my last time trying to get you these letters."

It was a whole stack of letters from Matt. Some from two years ago. The latest one from three months ago.

He hadn't forgotten me.

17

I started with the most recent letter.

Autumn,

I can only accept that your silence means that you have decided not to take the risk. I was hoping things could be different, but I understand. I haven't talked to Keith or Rachel about any of this. I figured you wouldn't want anyone meddling in this, and to be completely honest, I'm a little embarrassed to tell them that I wrote 30 letters to a girl whose picture I saw years ago and who I met for one day. I still can't explain to anyone why that one day meant so much, but it did. I won't be writing any more letters; but know that you'll be in my prayers and thoughts. -Matt

All this time he thought I was rejecting him and I thought he was rejecting me. I flipped through the postage stamps and found the earliest letter.

I took a month to think about that risk. My mind hasn't changed. When I was in college, Keith would always tell me about you. He'd tell me how I should move to Miami to meet this girl called Autumn who was funny and could play both the piano and guitar and make up a song about anything. I wasn't really game for his matchmaking. But then, I figured, hey why not, when he asked me to be the best man for his wedding. But, I just couldn't get a release as much as I tried. When Keith sent me the wedding pictures, I asked him who the girl with the pasted-on smile was. I don't know why I found it comical and endearing that while everyone was happy, I could tell from your picture that you were only trying to be. Keith told me it was you. The girl he'd been telling me about for years. Every time I'd call, I'd ask about you, but then he told me you and Rachel barely talked anymore. So, I stopped asking as much. But, then when he told me about the baby shower, he mentioned that you were going to be there. To be honest, I knew Keith was going to make sure you got picked to be my partner for the game. Naturally, he would, and I wasn't mad at that. I wanted to meet you.

Dinner that night was even better than I thought it would be. I felt like I could be 100% myself and I knew you were being yourself too. I wouldn't mind accompanying you on all those trips and this may be too strong, but I'm totally cool with the orchard and you deciding the names, except maybe Maria is better than Mary. You seem like every prayer I've said for all these years, even with the self-sabotage.

I've never said that to anyone. No, for real, I'm not lying. I don't know what happened in the past. But, I do want you to know that I would never intentionally try to hurt you. So, Autumn, will you take that risk with me?

I kept opening up letters. One was in June of the last year when I first got to Michigan.

We arrived in Spain yesterday. Not the city, we've been mostly staying the countryside. I actually prefer it out here because there's so many stars. I remember when I was younger my mom would tell me no matter how far apart we were that we were under la misma luna y estrellas (the same moon and stars). It's so quiet at night and I finally feel like I can hear. Not sure if that makes sense to you.

"It makes perfect sense to me," I said quietly. I continued reading.

It's been a year and I haven't heard back, and I feel stupid to keep writing to you. You're the one that insisted on these letters and I've actually been enjoying writing them. It's comforting to write them, even though I'm not sure if you're even reading them at this point. I now understand all the other soldiers who write home to their families and friends. When you talk, you wait for someone to fill the gaps and not make it awkward. When you have to send a letter, you have time to share everything you're saying without interruption and so you know when you get back a letter they're getting the same opportunity.

So tonight, I'm looking up at the sky saying a prayer for you knowing that you're under la misma luna y estrellas.

Normally, I would've run for my phone and called Rachel and Ellie but instead I grabbed my keys and raced to Sister Blossom's house.

18

I pulled up to Sister Blossom's house. I went to knock on the door when I noticed that her blinds were open, and the house looked empty. Empty, as in no furniture. I felt my heart start racing. Had someone robbed Sister B?

I went to grab my phone when I saw a stack of letters peeking out under her doormat. One had my name on it and the others were addressed to Ellie, Rachel, Camila and Valentina.

I opened mine.

If you've opened this I know that you have finally seen your bamboo and my time with you has come to an end. Yes, bamboo may seem dead, but they're more alive than you know. They're working beneath the soil, doing much more than you can see. You needed my message the most Autumn, and the Father chose this particular plant to show you how to hold on when nothing seems to be happening. But, the bamboo makes up for any lost time. The work the Father sent me to do with you is now complete, but your journey is far from over. You may think that your prayer was the bamboo, and I suppose it is. But, you are the bamboo. You will grow so much in the days, weeks, months, and years to come. There is so much for you to experience. I look forward to worshipping with you one day. I know the sound of the redeemed will be much more glorious than mine. Here are some more seeds, I can't tell you what they are, but give them to someone else someday who needs them. You'll know when you've met them. I look forward to seeing them bloom as well.

I didn't give out that seed right away. I spent years planting some more seeds of my own. Matt and I married just months after that in the orchard in fall with the trees beautifully providing most of the decoration we needed. It was fast, but, hey, when you know, you know. Ellie, Rachel, Camila and Valentina were my bridesmaids. Isaac and Isaiah were my ring bearers and Rachel's baby girl, Brielle, was my flower girl. Well, she was too little to really throw flowers, so she had to get a little bit of help. It was just 30 of our closest friends and family and it was perfect. God really did make everything beautiful in his time.

Matt wasted no time in getting my songs copyrighted and sent out to as many people as possible. Those songs became pretty popular and I spend most of my days writing, sharing my testimony and the gospel. I didn't tell many people about who Sister Blossom really was. I didn't think I even truly knew who she was. Just like her letter said, that I still keep with me today, we'll find each other again.

We didn't waste much time either having kids. I now have Joshua who's recently become a teenager and thinks he knows everything, Caleb, his dad's shadow, and Maria, who's got her dad wrapped around her finger. With our expanding family, we eventually had to leave my townhouse which was one of the hardest decisions for me, not because I was attached to the house, but because I couldn't let go of the bamboo growing in the back. Matt had arranged for it to be uprooted and planted in our new home. That was one of the best surprises ever.

Rachel's boys are now about seventeen and Brielle is

fifteen. Saints pray for her please. She gave her seeds away to a ten-year-old little girl, Lisa, in foster care that had started attending Harvest. She'd been removed from another foster home where she was being sexually assaulted. Lisa planted those seeds and prayed every day for a family to adopt her, and as her daisies grew, so did Rachel and Keith's love for her. Keith and Rachel adopted her about a year after she started going to the church. Lisa was now trying to decide which offer to accept: Harvard or Yale.

Ellie moved out to California with Jesse after they got married. After a couple years of waiting and trusting, they had a girl and a boy named Hope and David. Ellie's seeds went to Emmy. Aloe came from the ground, but I think the true healing balm was the renewed closeness of sisters. Emmy moved out west with Ellie and went back to school for a counseling degree and now works as an interventionist for addicts.

Camila and Valentina both still live in New York, Valentina now owns two brands. Blossom for women. Titus for men. Camila runs the business while Valentina pumps out the designs. Valentina had given them to a guy in grad school who looked like he was having difficulty figuring out his path in life. He'd been kind of confused by the whole planting thing, but he'd done it. Most likely just to impress Valentina. Well, he figured it out, because they ended up marrying. She now keeps up with those strawberries growing outside their home, and he runs the legal affairs of her business.

Camila gave us all a laugh when she told us how she'd gotten her seeds stolen in a train station. They had been in her purse.

"Man, I can cancel those cards, but I can't get back those seeds," she had said. But, she did. A week later, a homeless woman approached her, apologizing for stealing her purse. Everything was still in there. She said it was the scripture inside that bag of seeds that made her return it all. It held the same scripture about envy that Camila had gotten. Camila had given her the seeds. But, get this, the seeds weren't ivy. They were beautiful pink roses.

Turns out, the homeless lady, Joanna, had a business degree and had a pretty good job working as an investment banker. But, she had a gambling problem that had ruined her career and family. She had been too proud to tell her family that she was out on the streets. They'd lost contact with her because she had no cell phone.

Camila helped her get back in contact with her son and daughter. She even got her a job again. Joanna took a liking to the whole growing roses thing and grew all the roses for Camila's wedding to her son Joseph five years ago.

God really has a sense of humor.

After 15 years, I still hadn't given out my seeds. It's not that I didn't want to. It's just that I knew I wanted to wait for the right person. There were times I thought it could've been a woman I'd met on a trip to India who'd grown weary of waiting for her parents to come to Christ, or one back home in Michigan who'd lost her husband in a car accident. There were so many others that I thought could be the right person. But every time, I'd get ready to give it to them, something deep down would let me know they were not the person for this particular seed. They needed my prayers, my presence, or even my financial gifts, but not the seeds I held in my bag every day, waiting for the right person.

I found her at a wedding I was invited to by someone who told me they'd been inspired by my story. She was standing next to the bride, tears springing in her eyes as the couple recited their vows. Only I knew who those tears were really for. I couldn't keep my eyes off of her for the rest of the day. Her pasted on smiles and feigned happiness dissolved into a somber stare as the couples danced on the floor at the reception.

I made my way over to her.

"If you leave now for the bathroom, you can avoid the bouquet toss altogether," I said.

She laughed. "Is that the trick?"

I held out my hand for her to shake. "Autumn Anderson."

Her eyes widened. "As in the singer? I saw your story about planting those seeds."

"I guess," I said. "To my kids, I'm just Autumn Anderson, the dishwasher. My kids aren't too much into planting seeds."

She grinned, and I continued. "Instead of moping at a wedding, I have a challenge for you."

She looked like she was going to get defensive, but instead she asked, "What kind of challenge?"

"I have some seeds here. Plant them and tell me all that you learn about yourself."

"Are they bamboo like yours?"

"Here's the thing," I said. "I don't know what they

are. But they're yours." I wrote down my phone number on a piece of paper and slid it to her. "I want to hear all about the process. What the plant is, isn't as important."

She took the bag from me and put them in her clutch purse. "Do you usually just give women seeds to plant?"

"No," I said. "I've held on to this bag for fifteen years waiting for the right person."

"Why me?"

I smiled.

"Because heaven is waiting for you to bloom."

ABOUT THE AUTHOR

Shaida Escoffery is the author of several books including Idle, Wild, Love, and Grace Found Me. Born in Brooklyn, NY and raised in Miami, FL, she is the alumna of both the University of Miami and New York University's Graduate School.